THE BLESSINGS JAR

BY
LOREE LOUGH

No part of this publication may be reproduced, stored in a retrieval system, or transmitted in any form or by any means, electronic, mechanical, photocopying, recording, or otherwise, without the written permission of the publisher.

Text Copyright © 2022 Loree Lough
All rights reserved.

Published 2022 by Progressive Rising Phoenix Press, LLC
www.progressiverisingphoenix.com

ISBN: 978-1-958640-25-8

Printed in the U.S.A.

Edited by Mary Alford

Cover photo: "Amish Buggy in Winter stock photo" by David Arment, iStock Photo ID: 1029542260, used under license from iStock.com.

Cover design by Amanda Thrasher and William Speir

Book design by William Speir
Visit: http://www.williamspeir.com

CHAPTER 1

Splashes of vermillion, amber, and gold painted the Alleghenies' peaks. *Oh, to have time to duplicate* that *on a canvas,* Anna thought, closing the plantation shutters.

Polly, who'd been a regular at *Let's All Eat* for as long as Anna could remember, unshielded her eyes.

"Oh, thank you, dear! The sunset is beautiful… but at this time of day, it tends to glint from things like the chrome napkin holders, doesn't it?"

Anna's mother rolled up, locked her wheelchair beside Polly's table, and pointed at the white shutters. "I still do not understand why you replaced perfectly good roller shades with those dust collectors."

"Dust?" Elmer said. "I defy you to find any!"

Ella stood behind their mother. "*Daed* is right. Plus, those dingy old shades made the place feel dark and dreary."

Fannie silenced her husband and youngest daughter with a hard stare.

As usual, Ella ignored it. "Your ankles are swollen, *Maem*. Let me take you home, so you can put your feet up."

Almost instantly, the woman's annoyance transitioned to self-pity. "I can always count on my *good* daughter."

Ella sent an "I'm-sorry" look over their mother's head and grasped the wheelchair's handles. "*Daed*, are you ready to leave, too?"

"No. I will stay, help Anna close up, and get things ready for the breakfast rush." Patting his wife's hand, he said, "Is that is all right with you, *liebchen*?"

"My love, indeed," Fannie huffed. "Do as you please. *I* am going home."

Ella shrugged into her coat. "Let me warm up the van first. Can you believe the weather report?" She lowered her voice to imitate the announcer. "'Garrett County could wake up to six inches of snow tomorrow!'"

She was half in, half out the door when David swiveled on his counter stool to face her. "On my way in, I noticed a couple of icy spots, so—"

"What!" Fannie interrupted. "Just what we need. Some *Englisch*er slipping, breaking a hip, and suing us!"

"No worries," David said. "I opened the salt bucket Anna put beside the door and scattered some around."

"Thanks, David."

And as the door closed behind Ella, Fannie said, "That takes the cake. Now she has the customers doing her job!"

"Fannie, stop it. Stop it right now!"

It wasn't like her father to raise his voice, and Anna said a quick prayer that her mother wouldn't fuel his ire with a sarcastic retort.

"I cannot help it. She has time to rearrange the tables and chairs, and change the menu, and hire new people—all without asking our permission—but no time to protect our customers?"

"The poor girl works from dawn to dark, running this place, taking care of the house, taking care of *us*. You make no secret of how much you hate being in that chair," Elmer said, pointing at it. "Well, I do not like mine, either, but you do not hear me grumbling about it all the live-long day! You behave as though it is Anna's fault we have become helpless old people!"

Anna could think of a dozen words to describe the man her father had become since the accident, but helpless wasn't one of them. She was about to tell him so when Ella returned.

"That wind is positively wicked!" She grabbed Fannie's coat from the rack beside the door. While helping put it on, Ella said, "They were not kidding about that storm. It's snowing already, so I think you should come with us, *Daed*."

He gave it a moment's thought, and as Ella helped him into his jacket, Anna peered out the window. "Nature is so strange," she said, mostly to herself. "Just a few minutes ago, the sun was blinding us, but look at that sky now."

"I'll take you outside first, *Daed*. So sit tight for just a minute, *Maem*."

Anna reached for her own coat. "I will help you get them situated."

"No, you have plenty to do, right here. Anyway, getting them in and out is easy as pie, thanks to the extra money you paid for the lift."

"Will you stay the night? The spare room is clean, and Mouser would love to see you."

"That cat likes anyone who sneaks her a piece of cheese," Ella said and laughed.

Anna wanted her sister to say yes. Between caring for their parents, working to keep the wolf from the door, maintaining tidy houses and yards, the sisters hadn't had much time to enjoy one another's company in the two years since the accident.

"I will make popcorn and hot chocolate…"

"We'll see," Ella said.

In other words, she'd stay *if* their mother didn't give her a reason not to.

Anna topped off David's coffee. "The patience of a saint," she whispered, "that little sister of mine."

"Just like her big sister."

Could he hear her heart, thumping like a drum, from his side of the counter?

Isaac, his constant companion, said, "The beef stew was especially good tonight."

David tapped his bowl's rim. "I noticed that, too. Did you add something to the recipe?"

The Blessings Jar

As a matter of fact, she'd stirred in a spoonful of brown sugar. But with her mother so near, no doubt waiting for another excuse to pounce, she didn't dare admit it. "I'm glad you both enjoyed it."

He held her gaze, telling her without words that he was aware how challenging it could be, dealing with Fannie's cranky conduct. Why couldn't he understand that she'd loved him nearly all of her life!

If she continued gazing into his eyes like a lovestruck schoolgirl, someone was bound to notice. *Someone like your mother.* The idea jarred her, and she carried the coffee carafe to Polly's table.

The elderly woman held a hand over her mug. "Oh, no thank you, dear. It'll keep me up all night."

"Because despite what I taught her, she puts too many grounds into the basket."

Polly frowned at Fannie. "If you ask me, her coffee—like everything in the diner *these days*—is always perfect."

Had her mother picked up on the way Polly had emphasized *these days,* a not-so-subtle insinuation that things had been less than perfect before Anna accepted the management role?

The woman patted Anna's hand. "I'll take the check instead, because you are right, that sky seems threatening. Hard to believe a woman like me, born and bred in Oakland, is afraid to drive in the snow, but it is the truth!"

"I think it scares all of us a little."

Anna made her way back to the counter. A woman like me, Polly had said. *A woman like you would probably never mistreat those who love you, not even if a horrible accident put you into a wheelchair.*

Instantly, she felt terrible. It was unfair, unchristian, and wrong to judge her mother's actions. *There but for the grace of God…*

David called her name, rousing her from self-censure.

"Will you give Isaac and me some of your lemon meringue pie?"

She'd give him her *heart,* if only he'd ask!

Anna plated up two slices and slid one to Isaac. As David accepted the second, his fingers brushed hers. The touch didn't last longer than a blink. More than long enough to send her heart into high gear. Again.

When Polly opened the door to leave, a blast of cold air blew into the diner.

Ella shivered. "Did someone turn the calendar page without telling

The Blessings Jar

me? It should not be this cold in September."

Fannie heaved an impatient sigh. "What a silly thing to say, Ella. You've lived every one of your twenty-five years here."

"I was teasing, *Maem*."

Anna sent her sister a sympathetic smile and felt a little sorry for herself, too, since that last criticism had probably convinced Ella not to spend the night. Not that she blamed her. If Anna could escape their mother's sharp tongue in a quaint little cottage…

The image of Ella, creeping away from the house, lifted her spirits.

"You should do that more often," David said.

"Do what?"

"Smile. It becomes you."

She was trying to think of a sensible reply when Ella announced, "Well, we're off."

Their mother huffed. "And not a moment too soon. If I have to watch these two, fawning over one another for another minute, I might—"

"Fannie…" Elmer scolded.

Sarcasm rang loud in her reply: "El-*mer*…"

Ella wasted no time getting Fannie into the van.

Now, only Isaac and David remained, eating pie at the counter.

"Delicious," David said around a bite.

Seeing his contentment filled her with joy. All too often, she'd watched him stare into space, looking anything but content.

She understood *why*.

As a girl, she'd sneaked into the schoolhouse after dark, hoping to find a misplaced book. What she'd found instead, haunted her, still.

Although David had done a masterful job these many years, hiding dark memories behind a friendly façade, Anna knew the truth.

And loved him all the more because of it.

∼

Side by side, David and Isaac made their way to his pickup truck.

"She is real pretty, don't you think, Davey?"

He despised the nickname, except when Isaac used it. "Who?"

Chuckling as he buckled his seatbelt, Isaac said, "You can't fool me. I saw you, starin' all moony-eyed the whole time we were at the diner. Same way you stare *every* time we're at the diner."

The Blessings Jar

Better be more careful from now on, Baden. Because if Isaac noticed, Fannie might. And only the good Lord knew what manner of torture the woman might inflict on poor Anna if that happened.

"Well, I'm right, right?"

"Yeah, she is pretty." An understatement, in David's opinion. He didn't think he'd ever seen bigger, greener eyes or longer, thicker eyelashes, or a smile that had the power to light up a dark room and brighten even his darkest moods.

"She's nice, too. And generous. Always making sure we have plenty of food."

That, too, was an understatement. Since she'd taken over management of the diner, the portions had all been large, and it hadn't escaped his notice that Anna made sure to deliver a little extra to him and Isaac.

"You ask me, I think she's sweet on you."

David's grip tightened on the steering wheel. *I didn't ask.*

"Nah," he said. God willing, that would be the end of it. But he knew better. He'd known better for a long time, starting at the after-services gathering years ago, when she'd sent her friend Charity to find out if he recognized her. She'd been fourteen, he, in his early twenties. So he'd set aside flattery, feigned shock, and said, "Who? That little girl over there?" To this moment, he felt like a heel, remembering the way she'd blushed as her lips formed a little O, right before her big eyes filled with tears... and she ran from the church basement.

"What do you think?"

"About what?"

"Do *you* think Anna is sweet on you?"

"Isaac, how many times have we talked about this?"

"I dunno, 'bout a hunnert?" He wrinkled his nose. "Sorry, Davey."

"Nothing to be sorry for, m'friend." How many times had he said *that* in the past ten years?

A head injury, sustained in his early teens, had stunted Isaac's mental and emotional growth, but the big-hearted, hard-working fellow grew physically. At six-feet-four and two hundred seventy-five pounds, he gladly put his strength to use any time anyone needed help. If David lived to the age of Moses, he didn't think he'd forget the day, more than ten years ago, when Isaac's parents announced that

The Blessings Jar

an Indiana cousin needed help with his struggling farm. They would move to Nappanee, they'd said, but couldn't afford to take their eldest son. The Stolls' reaction to his sorrowful pleas? "The Lord will provide. He always does." Disbelief, and overwhelming pity, compelled David to offer a room and a paycheck at Red Oak Farm, and Isaac had been with him ever since.

"Think she ever gets tired?"

"Anna? Sure. Everyone grows weary."

"'Member the way she hired Max and Dan to fix up her house? So her mother and father wouldn't have to climb stairs after the accident?"

Yes, he remembered.

"An' how she quit teaching to take care of them?"

Yes, he remembered that, too.

Isaac exhaled a heavy sigh. "That was sad, 'cause she really, *really* loved teaching the children."

David also remembered the way she'd invested the remainder of her savings in her parents' struggling diner. New tables, chairs, windows and doors, a more efficient kitchen exhaust system... and most recently, bright plantation shutters to replace brittle, yellowing roller shades.

"Ella's nice, too, of course."

David's white mailbox came into view. It had become a local landmark, thanks to his mother's painting of a bushy red oak tree and Old West style letters that spelled out Red Oak Farm. David flicked the turn signal and slowed to make the turn into the long, winding drive.

"Not as pretty as Anna, but I would never say so, 'cause that might hurt her feelings. She has been nice to me."

It had always seemed to David that Isaac was sweet on Ella.

"Bet she would marry you, if you asked."

David snorted. "What do I need with a wife?"

"You do not *need* one, but wouldn't it be nice?"

Isaac unbuckled his seatbelt and pointed at the tree-lined drive. "I'm glad I planted silver maples instead of red oaks. They grow faster. Before long, these will be big enough to drive under. Like–like–like a tree tunnel!"

Thank You, Lord, David prayed, *for distracting him from talk of a wife*.

"Only…" Squinting, Isaac said, "Think that'd upset your mother?"

"I think she'd enjoy riding through a tree tunnel."

"No. I mean, if Anna was your wife, would your mother's feelings get hurt? On account-a she's kinda the woman of your house?"

It wasn't something David had ever considered, because marriage—especially to someone like Anna—was out of the question.

"Cash is here to meet us!"

The friendly, clumsy German shorthaired pointer hadn't missed a meeting since David brought him home five years ago. The dog loped alongside the truck, and when David parked, Cash galloped around to the passenger side.

"There's my buddy," Isaac said, squatting. Cash rolled onto his back and flashed a big doggy smile as Isaac scratched his belly.

David leaned on the pickup's hood. "Need I remind you," he said to the dog, "that *I'm* the one who saved you from that abusive breeder?"

"Uh-oh. You hurt Davey's feelings," Isaac teased. "Better pay him some attention."

The dog's round, golden eyes connected with David's, as if seeking proof. Within seconds, Cash sat at his feet and, crouching, David drew him close.

"I'm glad you saved him, Davey, and I think he is, too."

David absorbed Cash's affection, pretty much the only physical contact he allowed himself to share with another living being. How much sweeter would it be, he wondered, holding Anna in his arms?

"Does Anna have a dog?"

"I have heard her talk about a cat…"

"Oh, yeah. That tabby she found, hanging around behind the diner." Isaac snickered. "'Member how she named it Mouser, 'cause she thought it might catch mice? And the way she sometimes calls it Lazy, and says it probably wouldn't recognize a mouse if it saw one?"

Memory of the way she'd looked, sharing the story, inspired warmth that started in his chest and coursed through his veins.

"Think Mouser and Cash could be friends?"

What a peculiar question…

"Y'know, in case you ever *was* to marry Anna, and they had to live together?"

The Blessings Jar

Much as David hated to admit it, Isaac had painted a pretty picture: The two of them, whiling away the hours, Cash at their feet and Mouser in her lap...

Straightening, David slapped a hand to the back of his neck. *Get hold of yourself, fool. No good can come from wanting impossible things.*

"Supper in fifteen minutes," his mother called through the screen door.

Isaac caught up to him, said in a rough whisper, "We gonna tell her that we already ate at the diner?"

"That might upset her." *Might?* He'd learned the hard way that it *would*.

To hear Charlotte tell it, painstaking hours went into every meal—hours that kept her from other household chores—filling the big stainless pot with melted lard, water, a mystery blend of spices, and canned meats and vegetables. Too bad all that effort resulted in lumpy stew, dried-out roasts, and watery soups. One glance at the shed door reminded him of the night, a few months back, when his brother tapped a front tooth. "It's loose," he'd whispered, "thanks to *Maem*'s biscuits. Bet they'd knock a man unconscious!" When Isaac said they weren't *that* bad, Ethan invited him outside, and hurled one at the shed. The dent was still clearly visible from all the way across the yard.

"So, what is the plan this time, then?"

How sad that, in order to protect his mother's feelings, David, his father and brother, and Isaac, too, had to decide ahead of time whether they'd choke down the unpalatable food or hide it under a napkin… and volunteer to clean up. He suppressed a laugh, because he couldn't remember the last time his mother had cleared the table or washed the dishes.

"If you married Anna, we wouldn't need a plan, on account-a *she* can cook."

Yet again, Isaac's simple words conjured a scene: Anna, delivering bowls of mouth-watering food to the table, then sitting across from him, inviting him to pass mashed potatoes and gravy.

But dreams like that, he reminded himself, were for teenage girls, not grown men.

Especially not men like you.

CHAPTER 2

"Morning, Broze. Ready for your treat?"

The turkey didn't seem to mind the inch of white stuff that covered the ground. It purred, puffed out its chest, and like a fat, feathery pup, waited for a morning snack. David reached into his shirt pocket and withdrew a tiny box of raisins. Crouching, he shook the contents into a cupped palm and waited as Broze accepted them, one at a time.

Turkey farming would never make him rich, but he loved everything about it, from the up-at-five to shepherding birds back to the barns at dusk. Of all the available breeds, he'd opted for the Narragansett. Smaller than the Bronze, White, or Auburn varieties, their intelligence, hardiness, and calm dispositions more than made up for what they lacked in weight. He'd chosen wisely, as evidenced by hundreds of satisfied return customers, who'd found Red Oak Farm through word of mouth and claimed, "Never roasted a turkey that tasted as good!"

Broze pressed closer and as every morning, David obliged his invitation to smooth the soft black feathers. While courting a hen, the bird would fluff up to show off the bright white chest that highlighted his blue and red head and thick, alternating black and white layers.

"Who's a pretty bird?"

Broze replied with another purr, and as David crossed the fenced-in pen, followed like a devoted pup.

He latched the gate behind him and joined his mother on the snow-covered pea gravel path.

"Do you have a minute?"

"For you? I have two," he teased.

Charlotte pulled her shawl tighter around her shoulders. She wasn't smiling when she said, "We need to make some changes."

A new pot to replace one she'd burned, instead of the new-fangled clothes dryer she'd been hinting about?

"No. This is farm related."

At last count, twenty-eight Pleasant Valley men worked for Red

The Blessings Jar

Oak Farm, each with interchangeable skills: The list of turkey predators included coyotes and raptors, rats and snakes, weasels, bobcats, foxes, and more. So, in addition to their normal duties, his brother Ethan, Isaac, and a handful of others made regular inspections of the pens and barns, and made immediate repairs to fencing and foundation cracks created by nature and determined killers. A few helped David oversee the breeding, hatching, and brooding processes, while others manned the processing plant. Robert Baden's natural people skills made his father a valuable asset in the sales office. So far, though, Charlotte's particular business acumen remained undiscovered.

Leaning his backside against the gate, he waited for her to explain.

"You need to fire Michael Josephs."

"What? Why?"

She shivered. "He is… creepy."

He pictured the man: Short, paunchy, bespectacled, with a balding, too-big-for-his-body head. David had never been particularly fond of the guy, who frequently arrived late for work or left early, took unapproved shortcuts that disrupted production, and found countless ways to shift his responsibilities onto others' shoulders. Dominated by his wife and teenage daughter, the man exercised his *I-am-my-own-man* muscles on the job, which caused resentment among coworkers. Twice, David had taken him aside to deliver friendly yet no-nonsense reprimands. Both times, the man had begged for another chance; without the job, how would he keep Katerina and Elizabeth satisfied? Pity—and the Amish tradition of accepting others' flaws as the Almighty accepts our own—compelled David to take the man at his word. Still…

"Creepy isn't a firing offense, *Maem*."

Charlotte pursed her lips. "But, son. He *stares*. All the time. At…" Blushing, she added, "…in a completely inappropriate way, and at completely inappropriate things. And before you say it's all in my mind, you should know that others agree."

"Others?"

"Fannie Hertzler, for one. Why, just last Sunday, she asked me to turn her wheelchair around because he was ogling her…"

She shivered again, and something told him the temperature had nothing to do with it.

The Blessings Jar

"...in *that way*. Fannie says he stares at her daughters the same way."

The idea that any man might look at his mother—*and at Anna!*—in such a way caused both fists to curl at his sides.

"I will have a word with him."

"For your information, Elmer Hertzler already had a word with him."

"And?"

"And, as one would expect from a man like that, he laughed it off. Told Elmer that women get the attention they crave by making a drama out of everything, and when that doesn't work, they *lie*."

Yes, since the accident, no one dared rile Anna's mother, but she'd always been honest, sometimes to a fault. And yes, his own mother had her cantankerous moments too, but she'd cut off her yard-long braid before she'd stretch the truth. How dare the man call her a liar!

"I will ask for God's guidance in the matter."

Charlotte's eyes narrowed. "That's what you said when the know-it-all's sneaky tinkering broke the deboning machine."

It was true.

"You said it again when he lied about sanitizing the conveyors. If you hadn't already earned the trust of the safety inspector, that lie might have cost you hundreds in fines. And a shutdown!"

True again.

"He is a threat to your business. Your employees deserve better, and so do you!"

"You have my word. I will pray about it."

She grasped his hands, gave them a slight shake. "So will I."

"Thank you," David said, turning toward the office.

"Where are you going?"

"I need to return a few calls and balance the checkbook, then make a quick trip to the bank." And on the way home, he'd stop at *Let's All Eat*, see what kind of pie Anna had baked that morning. If that couldn't improve his mood, nothing could.

"I'm making my special chicken and dumplings for supper…"

His stomach tensed at the memory of the last time she'd served it. As a teen, Charlotte had suffered an upper respiratory infection that left her with a susceptibility to lung ailments… and a permanent loss of taste and smell. She worked hard to keep up with household chores

The Blessings Jar

while adding to the family coffers with vegetables—fresh in season, canned, the rest of the year—sold from the roadside stand she'd built with her own two hands, so her husband and sons, and Isaac, too, good-naturedly consumed every bland, or over-spiced, or burnt concoction.

"Wipe that 'please, no!' expression from your face." She drilled a bony finger into his chest. "I have turned over a new leaf. Starting today, I'll measure ingredients and follow the cooking instructions to the letter. Why didn't I think of it sooner!"

His stomach relaxed, then tensed again. It hadn't fully recovered from last night's cabbage soup. Without his mother's poor cooking to justify eating at the diner, what excuse would he use to see Anna?

"Well, don't just stand there all sad-eyed, like a lost pup," Charlotte said. "The sooner you finish your bookwork, the sooner you can have that talk with Michael."

Together, they walked toward the office. "What's on your schedule this afternoon?" he asked.

"My shop needs a new sign, and I'm going to make one."

"If it can wait until the weekend, I'll do it for you."

"Thanks, son, but no thanks. I love working with tools, and this will give me a chance to see if my artistic skills are still intact."

"Aw, it hasn't been long since you picked up a paintbrush. Why, just day before yesterday, Isaac hung another of your decorated, hand-bent stars on the fence out front."

Every fence post boasted one of her creations. On some, she'd painted livestock, on others, field flowers, great horned owls perched on loblolly pines, and more.

"They're all beautiful, but in my opinion, that sunset over Backbone Mountain is your best work, by far."

"They will do… considering I used exterior paint, so the pictures would stand up to foul weather." She exhaled a girlish sigh. "If only I had been blessed with a talent for watercolors, like Anna. Hers are so lovely!"

Charlotte aimed a wistful glance toward the shed-turned-studio where she created artful crafts that appealed to locals and tourists alike. "I realize the poor girl has been busy since the Hertzlers' accident. I *still* pray for the strength to forgive the drunkard who put them both in wheelchairs."

The Blessings Jar

Forgiveness… one of the most difficult things about living Plain. It was the reason Anna's parents refused to press charges, allowing the man to immediately return to his normal life instead of serving years for driving while intoxicated. And it had shrouded David like a dirty spiderweb since—

"I'm sure that between taking care of Fannie and Elmer, the house and the diner, Anna doesn't have much time to herself, but… does she make time to paint?"

The question roused David from dark memories. "How would I know?"

Her left brow rose in response to his cranky tone. "Well, you see her several times a week, so…"

He cleared his throat. "At the diner. I order a meal. She delivers it. The subject of art never comes up."

Charlotte's voice changed from conversational to mildly suspicious. "If you say so." She tugged at her shawl again. "I pray she makes time for it now and then, because she's too talented to hide all that beauty under a bushel."

All it took was the word *beauty* to conjure her pretty, always-smiling face.

"When you see her later, give her my best." She followed the flagstone walkway he'd installed between the pens and the house, leaving tiny boot prints in the snow. Stopping a few yards away, she said, "May God guide your words as you talk with Michael."

He'd fired only one other man, for drinking on the job. He'd genuinely liked Tim Martins, so it hadn't been easy. Showing Josephs the door shouldn't be quite as difficult, all things considered.

Head down, David made his way to the office. He'd never liked balancing the checkbook, but today, God willing, it would serve as a much-needed distraction from the "creepy" matter.

He'd much rather spend the time discussing watercolor paintings at the diner.

~

A sliver of moonlight sneaked under the window shade and slanted across Anna's face. Squinting, she knuckled her eyes and rolled onto her back. The glowing green hands of the windup clock on her bedside table pointed to four and ten. Tossing the covers aside, she threw

The Blessings Jar

her legs over the edge of the mattress and, kneeling beside the bed, whispered, "Thank You, Father, for another day. Keep me from careless thoughts and words, and let me see things—good and bad—that come my way as opportunities. Bless me with patience to care lovingly for *Maem* and *Daed*. Provide all of Your children's needs, whatever they may be."

Upon opening her eyes, Anna saw her blessings jar, standing in a pool of silvery light on her dresser top. The last tiny, folded slip of paper she'd placed into the jar last night must have opened, because even from ten feet away, she saw David's name.

Padding across the braided rug, she unscrewed the jar's lid, and quietly read, "'David thinks I have a becoming smile. I am blessed!'"

Enclosing it in a fist, she pressed it to her chest and pictured his sturdy frame, long-lashed eyes, sandy waves…

But daydreaming was no way to start the day. Re-creasing the paper, she dropped it atop dozens just like it and replaced the lid. On the way to the bathroom to wash and dress for the day, Anna stopped to peer out the window. Mouser walked a figure-eight around her ankles, purring and chirruping. Anna stooped to pet the cat. "Yes, little one, you'll have breakfast soon."

At the window again, she saw the carpet of sparkling white that hid the lawn, the walkway and drive, and covered the boxy black van.

"And to think I almost didn't pay extra for four-wheel drive!" she muttered, and dropped the curtains back into place.

After making her bed and twisting her hair into a tight bun, Anna tiptoed downstairs, shoes hanging from her fingertips. The instant her stockinged feet hit the floor, her father looked up from his Bible.

"*Guten morgen*, Anna. Did you sleep well?"

Tousled hair and beard, and the fact that he'd moved from bed to wheelchair to recliner told her he'd spent another restless night.

Anna sat on the center couch cushion. "I slept like a baby." Winking, she pulled on her boots. "That isn't true. Babies are up every two hours, and I didn't wake until just a few minutes ago."

Elmer chuckled. "Ah, *süßes mädchen*, your happiness is contagious!"

She loved that he still called her *sweet girl*… when they were alone and safe from Fannie's stern lecture: "Pet names are rooted in vanity, and vanity is sinful!"

The Blessings Jar

"I need to feed Mouser," she said. And as if on cue, the cat leaped into Elmer's lap.

"She is rumbling like a well-oiled motor," he teased, scratching between the pointy, striped ears.

After feeding the animal, Anna grabbed her coat.

"You filled the wood box last night," Elmer said.

"And now I need to shovel a path to the woodpile."

"Yes, I looked out the window and saw the snow, but Anna, it is dark outside still."

"Ah, but the moon is shining like a beacon."

She had no idea how long he'd been awake, but remembering how much he enjoyed that first cup of morning coffee, Anna darted into the kitchen to start a pot. God willing, the walk and drive would be snow-free by the time it finished perking.

"It will only take a few minutes," she said, one hand on the doorknob.

"A few cold and backbreaking minutes." Elmer hung his head. "If only I could help you with such things. I hate being so useless!"

At least twice a day since his release from the hospital, her once-strong, capable father had said similar words. And nothing she'd said had convinced him he was anything but useless. Anna went to him, pressed a kiss to his temple. "Are you forgetting that you took care of Ella and me for decades?"

A sob formed in her throat, or she would have cited examples: Risking life and limb to hang side-by-side swings from the high branches of the ancient oak out front. Building step stools because "no *tochters* of mine will struggle to get into their little beds." When Fannie was busy—or in a foul mood—he'd good-naturedly helped with bonnet and apron ties, and despite long hours to keep the diner afloat, her father had always made time to help his girls with homework.

"If not for your mother and me, you'd have a husband to do such things, to take care of *you* for a change. Someone like David."

David…

At fourteen, Anna began writing her dreams on thin strips of paper and deposited each in her blessings jar… along with every disappointment felt when he seemed not to notice her at church or community gatherings. Back then, she'd blamed their eight-year age gap, but

The Blessings Jar

with maturity, Anna came to realize that his past—not their age difference—explained his standoffishness. Lately, her jar held prayers... prayers that God would help David see that—

"It will be daylight soon," Elmer said, "and you have much to do before you leave for the diner." He patted her mittened hand. "Sorry you had to witness my whining."

"I didn't hear any whining. What I heard was proof that you got up too early. Just as soon as I've cleared the walk and drive, I'll fill your belly so full of pancakes and sausage gravy that it'll think it's Thanksgiving."

He chuckled. "A nice long nap sounds good."

She kissed his forehead and hurried outside, where the moon still glowed bright in the deep purple early-morning sky. With each pass of the shovel, Anna exposed more of the brick-lined flagstone walk, then used the tool as a plow blade, pushing snow from one side of the driveway to the other. Soon, the sun would rise, and with it, the temperature. By the time she left for *Let's All Eat*, the warmth would have melted any remaining snow, right down to the gravel.

After stomping slush from her boots and brushing snowflakes from her shoulders, Anna carried her hat, mittens, and coat into the parlor. A few minutes beside the woodstove's heat would ensure everything would be dry before she left for the diner.

Her father had dozed off with his Bible open on his lap. Easing closer, Anna read the verse from Proverbs just beneath his thick forefinger: "'*A cheerful heart is good medicine, but a crushed spirit dries up the bones.*'"

"Your happiness is contagious," he'd said, apologizing for whining.

She'd never tell him that her so-called happiness took concentration, because much of the time, she felt anything *but* cheerful. It had been hard enough for her formerly-independent parents to accept help, but without hearing that verse every so often, the only things keeping Anna from falling apart were prayer and pride.

Once she'd cooked the pink out of the sausage, Anna made creamy white gravy and poured it into the skillet. She'd just mixed up a batch of pancake batter when Ella entered through the back door.

"Why won't nature make up its mind?" she said, hanging up her coat. "Is it winter or is it autumn?"

The Blessings Jar

"I agree. It was rather warm when I shoveled."

"Sausage gravy?" Ella asked, moving close to Anna's side.

"*Daed* didn't sleep well last night. Memories of the accident, I think. So, a special treat to boost his spirits."

Ella glanced into the parlor, where their father snoozed contentedly in his favorite chair. "He tries so hard to act like the paralysis doesn't bother him."

But both sisters knew better.

"If *Maem* behaved more like him, we'd all be so much better off!" Suddenly, Ella brightened. "Guess who I saw on the way here?"

Anna turned up the heat under the cast iron griddle.

"David, that's who. He was helping Phillip plow the roads."

She pictured him, bundled up against the cold, operating an enormous machine …

Anna stirred the pancake batter and hoped Ella would think the stove had caused the heat in her cheeks. "How are things out there?"

"No need to behave all nonchalant with me, sister dear." Ella gave her a sideways hug. "It's no secret that you have feelings for him."

Only because her friend Charity couldn't keep a secret if it was locked up in a steel box.

"To answer your question, things are fine out there." Ella paused. "How about if we trade vehicles today," she said, stepping up to the sink. "I'd like to take *Maem* and *Daed* to my shop today. A change of pace for them, and I can get started on my latest order." She washed her hands, and while drying them, said, "*Maem* was in such an ugly mood yesterday that I didn't get a chance to tell you about the *Englischer* who stopped by." Grabbing a stack of plates, she began setting the table. "Her wedding is only a few weeks off, and she needs a wedding gown. Wants me to make one for her maid of honor, too."

Ella's seamstress talents were known throughout Garrett County, so it was no surprise that customers returned time and again, often bringing friends and family. If the order had involved slip covers, a party dress or business suit, or draperies, excitement would have registered in Ella's voice. Instead, her tone was dull and matter-of-fact. Since the logging accident that took Abner from her, Ella had tried to avoid wedding-related jobs. As a widow with bills to pay, that wasn't always possible, so she focused on pleasing the brides-to-be. Once, several months after Abner's funeral, she'd told Anna that staying

The Blessings Jar

busy helped her miss him less. But even now, two years later, Anna wondered if Ella's broken heart would ever heal.

"You brought some of your design sketches, I hope?"

"Maybe next time." She glanced left, right, and lowered her voice. "I wasn't sure what kind of mood *Maem* might be in, and since *I'm* in no mood for her so-called helpful advice…"

"I understand."

"Guess I'd better wake her, huh?"

"Guess so."

"One good thing, we won't need to rouse *Daed* from his nap, because once she's up…"

Ella could have finished the sentence in any one of a dozen ways. *"…the complaining will begin."* Or *"…she'll tell us how we've disappointed her today."* As before, the harsh opinion filled Anna with shame, because only the Almighty knew how *she* might react to a life as a paraplegic.

"I have laid out her clothes," she told Ella. "If she balks at taking a bath, let her have her way. She had one last night, and unless she had an accident during the night—in which case, call me and I'll clean her up—there's no need for another this morning."

"I don't mind doing it."

"I know, but you'll be handling delicate fabrics later, so you'll want to stay fresh."

"Best sister ever!"

Smiling, Anna watched her round the corner on her way to their parents' quarters.

Before the accident, the space had been the parlor. While they were still in the hospital, Anna had hired Max to make the entire first floor wheelchair accessible. With the addition of a wall, the dining room became a parlor. He enclosed half of the covered porch and installed a bathroom and sunroom. Curtained French doors gave them privacy and access to the kitchen. Construction had eaten up nearly all of her savings, but Anna didn't mind. Seeing their self-confidence rise as they moved through the apartment, all on their own, was far more satisfying than the bank account that had been earmarked to buy a home of her own. If only Fannie would refrain from jumping at every opportunity to remind Anna that her name was *not* on the deed, or that her tinkering with the original floorplan had made the house suitable

The Blessings Jar

for a husband and children.

David seemed intent on spending the rest of his life alone. "So it's just as well…"

"What is just as well?"

Startled, she nearly elbowed the stack of pancakes from the counter.

"Oh, my," she said, laughing nervously, "I'm going to have to tie bells to your chair, *Daed*. I didn't hear you come in."

"Didn't mean to scare you. But maybe instead of putting bells on me to help your concentration, you ought to confront him."

"Confront him?" she echoed.

"Anyone can see how you feel about him… and how he feels about you." *Daed* held up one hand, as if taking an oath. "Now, now, I realize you are both busy, hard-working people, but have you asked yourselves how much easier your life might be with a partner at your side?"

Which should Anna react to first? That she'd let her feelings for David show, for all to see? That David had apparently been doing the same? Or whether to answer honestly… that she'd spent years, imagining—

"Who and why are you two talking partnership?" Fannie demanded.

It was a good thing she had a strong heart, because between the two of them sneaking up on her...

"I've made sausage gravy and pancakes, and I'm about to fry eggs, sunnyside-up, just the way you like them." Hiding her face in the refrigerator, she said, "Would you rather have milk or juice with your coffee?"

"When have you ever seen me drink milk? Or juice, for that matter?"

Ella, standing behind their mother, rolled her eyes, then filled two mugs with freshly-perked coffee. "I don't know about everyone else," she said, placing both on the table, "but I'm famished."

"See what happens when you don't do as your mother says?"

When Ella said, "You wake up hungry," there was no mistaking the strain in her usually smooth voice.

Fannie zeroed in on Anna. "Will you clear the snow from the walks and drive after you've cleaned up the breakfast dishes?"

The Blessings Jar

"The job is already done," Elmer said. "She finished while it was still dark."

"Well." Fannie sipped her coffee. "Good." Another sip, and then, "Now about this partnership. Why was I not consulted?"

"That is simple. It is not diner related," Elmer answered.

Frowning, she shook her head. And as understanding dawned, she gasped. "No. Not… not *David Baden*…"

She might as well have said *that… that Englischer!*

Other than herself, only three people knew that Anna had been guarding a secret, one that, if disclosed, could damage the peaceful, orderly façade David had assembled to help him forget…

…and Fannie was one of them.

Anna had just turned fifteen when she witnessed the horrible event. For two straight nights afterward, she'd paced her bedroom; for two straight days, she'd prayed: Should she tell someone about it? Sleep deprived and reeling from the shock of it, Anna had dropped a food-laden tray while helping out at the diner. Furious, Fannie had dragged her into the storeroom and demanded an explanation.

Afraid—for herself and for David—Anna blurted out the truth

about what she'd seen. Even now, fifteen years later, if she closed her eyes, Anna could still see the wide-eyed shock and revulsion on her mother's face.

She looked a little like that right now.

Please, Lord, don't let her say more!

CHAPTER 3

Once a week—sometimes twice—David inspected the turkey pens.

He'd used quality materials and paid careful attention to every detail when building each 75-foot by 75-foot enclosure, but nothing could prevent the slow damage from expansion and contraction caused by wind, precipitation, and temperature fluctuations. Gradual shifting also had a tendency to loosen interior roosts, as well as the wood-and-wire fencing that protected the birds from ground and airborne predators.

"What day is it?" Charlotte asked.

David turned, amazed that her voice had carried the hundred yards between the clothesline and the pens.

"It's Friday. Why?"

"Good!" After pinning a pillowcase to the line, his mother started walking toward him. "I asked your father to drive me to Oakland on Saturday." Flexing her fingers, she said, "Handling the wet clothes in the wintertime makes my hands ache."

He'd strung lines in the basement, where it was warm and dry. First, she'd complained they were too high. Once he'd lowered them, she'd said the ropes were sagging. He tightened them, and solved the *not-enough-lines* problem by adding more. By that time, David figured out that what his mother *really* wanted was an automatic clothes dryer. He would gladly have installed one... if his father hadn't said no.

"How'd you get *Daed* to change his mind?"

"I appealed to his sense of decency. 'If you want to wear decent clothes to town,' I said, 'you'll buy me a dryer.'"

It wasn't like Robert to give in without a fight, especially where modern conveniences were concerned.

"And he said yes, just like that?"

"Oh, he raised the usual objections, but I met them with common sense." She began counting on her fingers: "'You have a lawn mower,' I said, 'a chainsaw and a generator that lets you operate circular

The Blessings Jar

saws and drills.' He said, 'Those things help bring money into the house.' And I pointed out that *I* bring money into the house, too. And,' I said, 'after all my years of caring for you, am I not worth the cost of a dryer?'"

"Hard to argue with logic like that."

"True, but you know your father. I wouldn't put it past him to find some excuse to get out of taking me to town. 'We will go another day, soon,' he'll say."

She was probably right.

"If that happens, I'll take you."

"Thank you, son, thank you!"

Charlotte returned to the clothesline. "Fix this sight in your memory," she said over her shoulder. "You will not see me doing this again!"

Yes, he would, just as soon as springtime rolled around again, since she loved the scent of line-dried sheets, and the way sunshine kept the towels bright white. But why dampen her mood? She didn't ask for much and rarely came out on top of a disagreement with Robert Baden.

"Where is Isaac?" she asked. "There's a loose board on the back porch steps."

"He's repairing a gate. Just as soon as he's finished, I'll send him up to the house."

"What about Ethan?"

"I sent him to town for wood shavings for the pen floors."

"And your father?"

"Saw him last at breakfast." David grinned. "Why? You planning to remind him about the trip to town tomorrow?"

In place of an answer, Charlotte said, "I hope he *does* find an excuse to get out of it. Maybe then you will take me to lunch at the diner."

Even from this distance, he could see her sly smile. David didn't dare ask what she was up to.

"Are you aware that Anna Hertzler is terrified of birds?"

If it was true, David didn't know what it had to do with clotheslines and automatic dryers. *But if you're smart, you won't ask.*

"You heard the whole story? About the fisher cat attack, and the owl that saved her life?" She pinned a pair of his father's socks to the

The Blessings Jar

line. "Ridiculous, if you ask me, to fear birds when one came to her rescue."

"I should get back to work. Two more pens to check out."

Cash trotted up, and David squatted to rub the dog's head.

"Next time you see her, you should ask her to tell you all about it."

Maybe I will...

"Can you imagine it? One of those beasts, attaching itself to you, tooth and nail?"

While hunting, he'd seen one, and at first, mistook it for a weasel... until it darted up a tree and latched onto a squirrel. Instantaneous death was followed by a heinous, triumphant hiss. The memory made his neck hairs bristle, so no, he couldn't imagine what poor Anna had gone through.

And yes, he'd definitely ask her to tell him all about it.

Anna loved this time of day, when darkness hugged the house and the only sounds were the *tick* of the kitchen clock and the *squeak* of markers against calendar pages: Red for her parents' doctor and hospital appointments, green for social activities.

In the weeks following their release from the hospital, the squares glowed red with appointments for x-rays, scans and screenings, and blood draws to monitor their recovery. As the months turned into years, and Anna learned more about caring for two paraplegics, green dominated the pages.

Beneath October's colorful photograph of golden oak leaves, bold black letters said "Exercise and Massage." Anna didn't need a reminder to exercise their still-functioning muscles and massage those that didn't. As a teacher, Anna discovered that chalkboard messages helped cement lesson details in students' minds. The system also helped when Fannie objected to the work, allowing Anna to say, "Sorry, but it's on the calendar." One day, her mother would no doubt say, "Cross it out," and Anna would count on God to provide a response that put her mother back in a compliant mood.

She grasped the black pen to add Thomas Troyerson's funeral to tomorrow's block, but thought better of it. With snow flurries and temperatures in the low forties predicted, why risk colds or the flu—potentially dangerous ailments for people with compromised immune

The Blessings Jar

systems?

Returning the black marker to the cupboard drawer, Anna retrieved her satchel from the row of coat hooks near the back door and carried it to the table. The day planner inside had been a Christmas gift from her sister. She sat at the table and slid a hand over the buttery caramel-colored leather cover Ella had made for it, complete with hand-carved initials surrounded by curlicue vines and a tiny, whimsical butterfly.

Weeks ago, David had been at the diner counter when Anna penned a reminder in the Notes section.

"I've never seen one like that before," he'd said.

"A gift from Ella."

"She *made* it?" He'd held out a hand, hinting for closer inspection.

"Ella made it for me."

She slid it to him, and as his forefinger traced the A and the H, he'd said, "Beautiful, and since you can replace this year's pages with next year's, it's practical, too."

Hugging it to her chest, Anna sighed. *I need to add that smile of approval to my blessings jar!*

She opened the book and read her to-do list for the following morning: Help Matthew prep breakfast. Wrap silverware. Refill condiments containers.

Tomorrow was Luke's day off, meaning she'd need to make sure the restrooms were clean and put the trash out for pickup. If she set the alarm for four instead of four-thirty, she'd have plenty of time to get everything done before opening the doors at seven.

Would David stop by for his usual plate of flapjacks and sausage? Or would he and Isaac eat an early dinner, as they so often had? "Dinner," she said to herself. "It's less crowded and—"

Anna knew exactly why her thoughts so often turned to him.

One, she loved him. Loved everything about him, from his rugged good looks to his mellow voice to his boyish smile. Loved the way he'd rescued Isaac, and how he always seemed to be there for anyone who needed strong hands to repair wind-damaged roofs or a sturdy back to hoist hay bales.

And two, loving him made her feel guilty. If she could muster the courage to tell him what she'd seen—so that he wouldn't feel so alone and beaten-down by the secret—he might find real peace and

The Blessings Jar

happiness, finally!

"Please Lord," she whispered, closing the planner, "show me the way to help David."

Anna slid the book back into the tote, another beautiful handmade gift from her sister. This year, she intended to give something other than bolts of material, hooks-and-eyes, zippers, and spools of thread to restock Ella's supplies. The idea came to her during their last trip to the fabric store. After adding straight pins, buttons, and a roll of white lace to her handbasket, Ella had nearly drooled over a pair of shiny dressmaker's shears. At more than sixty dollars, they'd been out of her price range, so she'd put them back on the rack... and the very next day, Anna returned to the shop, alone, and bought them. She could hardly wait to see Ella's face when she unwrapped those scissors this Christmas!

Anna turned out the lights and went upstairs, and after getting ready for bed, sat at her desk to write up another slip for her blessings jar. *"Thank You, Lord, for blessing me with courage!"* On New Year's Day, she'd empty the jar, just as she had for so many years, read the messages that recounted her year, and give thanks for each blessing.

She screwed the lid onto the jar, set her clock, and climbed under the covers, and eyes closed, whispered, "The Lord is my shepherd, I shall not want…"

But she *did* want… David, as her husband, as the father of her children.

Tears filled her eyes, admitting for the thousandth time that God wouldn't answer her prayer until she did the right thing. *He might not answer even then, because you waited so long to do it.*

"But Lord, You know that I've *wanted* to tell him, that I've *tried* to tell him." Each time, fear had risen up and choked off her words, fear that he'd hate her for allowing him to suffer, alone, for so many years for no reason other than a gradually dimming hope that someday…

Mouser leaped onto the bed and snuggled close, and her purring lulled Anna to sleep. She woke feeling rejuvenated, ready to face this new opportunity to do what must be done…

…even if it meant snuffing out all chances of one day living her dream.

CHAPTER 4

"I promised Charlotte one of your peach pies."

Anna stopped in her tracks. "When?"

"Yesterday, when we met to work on her quilt."

"I hope she does not expect it soon," Elmer said. "Peaches are not in season."

"She will not mind canned."

"But then it won't be one of Anna's delicious pies."

"It will be, if she makes own crust."

When Fannie wanted something, logic had a way of bypassing her.

Eyes on Anna, she said, "I told her you would deliver it today. She is planning a special meal for Robert's birthday."

Today. With a diner full of hungry people and another early snowstorm approaching. Perhaps David would stop by, and she could send him home with one of the pies she'd baked this morning. But, much as Anna wanted to see him, she didn't… there hadn't been time since making her *do-the-right-thing* decision to find the right words.

"Oh, now I get it," Fannie said. "You're afraid to go over there because he raises turkeys, and turkeys are birds, and after all this time, you still have a ridiculous fear of anything that flies." She smirked. "I am surprised you tolerate butterflies and hummingbirds." She shook her head. "Feathers and beaks are the only things turkeys and owls have in common. Where is your faith that God will protect you?"

Anna had called on Him as the fisher latched onto her leg. As the owl swooped in, mighty wings beating her head and shoulders as sharp talons pierced her calf, trying to overpower its prey. Her father, seeing her bloody wounds, loaded her into his old truck, and sped to Garrett Regional. And as the ER staff cleaned and stitched up bites and scratches, prescribed powerful antibiotics, and administered the first of four painful rabies injections, each of which caused a swollen, achy upper arm and two days' worth of headaches and nausea. Anna asked herself—not for the first time—how much worse it might have been if she *hadn't* prayed for all she was worth?

The Blessings Jar

Memory of the attack had just begun to subside when her mother continued, "Besides, David's turkeys are in pens. As long as you stay *outside* the gates"—her voice took on the sing-songy tone adults often used when speaking to babies—"the big bad birds cannot get you."

"Fannie, your attitude is uncalled for," Elmer said. "Did you ever think to *ask* if Anna has time for this?" A frustrated sigh issued from him. "Do you ever stop and listen to yourself?"

From the look of things, Fannie was about to turn her wrath on Elmer, and to protect him from it, Anna said, "It's all right, *Daed*. I'll bake the pie and take it to Charlotte." Facing her mother, she tacked on, "And I'll be sure to tell her that *you* insisted on canned peaches."

Elmer winked and gave her the thumbs-up sign as she walked into the kitchen.

Matthew, standing at the eight-burner stove, said, "It's ready for your special touch." He put the lid on the big stainless soup kettle, then turned around. "Uh-oh, did I forget something at the farmer's market?"

"No, you bought everything we need, as always."

"Ahh, Fannie's on the rampage again, is she?" He moved to the griddle and slid the blade of a wide spatula under the sizzling bacon. "What's got her dander up this morning?"

Thanks to her mother, nearly everyone in Pleasant Valley had heard the story Fannie liked to call Attack Day, so Anna saw no point in avoiding the truth.

"She wants me to deliver a pie to Charlotte Baden." Opening a large jar of the peaches she'd canned during the summer, Anna said, "Today."

Matthew's nonchalant shrug said what words needn't: At one time or another, everyone in Pleasant Valley had witnessed—or been victim of—Fannie's mercurial mood swings. It was a shame, really, considering how the community had rallied to help out after the accident.

Odd, she thought, dumping the jar's contents into the colander, that Fannie had never aimed her verbal darts at David…

Ella joined them in the kitchen. "I couldn't help but hear all that, and I'm sorry, Anna. If I'd known the change in plans would spin her into a tizzy, I would have brought them to the shop."

"No apology necessary, li'l sister. You have a deadline to meet." She moved the peaches to a bowl and sprinkled cinnamon and brown

The Blessings Jar

sugar over them. Work had been Ella's saving grace; not only did it pay the bills, it protected her from their mother's abuse. After all the poor girl had already been through, she certainly didn't need that.

"The bride is bringing her maid of honor in for a fitting. Her mother, too."

In other words, having Fannie around, criticizing and complaining, wasn't good for business. Anna admitted that diner patrons were too busy chatting and eating to notice one woman, griping about the weather or wondering—out loud—why people didn't wipe their feet.

"I have half an hour before the ladies show up. Can I help with anything while I'm here?"

"Thank you, but no." Anna turned her to face the door. "Go home, use the time to relax. You deserve it!"

"I'll come back after the ladies leave. Your pie will be ready by then, and I can deliver it for you."

To protect her from being near hundreds of birds? Or the object of her unrequited love?

"You're a dear to offer, but I'll take care of it."

"But why, Anna, if you don't have to?"

She squared her shoulders. "It's the right thing to do."

Matthew and Ella exchanged a confused glance, and then Ella said, "All right, if you say so."

"Time's a-wastin'!"

"All right," she said again, "but I'll stop by after supper, help you get the folks ready for bed. And you can't talk me out of it."

This time, Anna gave her a playful shove. "Now go, before *Maem* finds an excuse to make you late."

The door had barely closed behind her when Matthew said, "She's some woman, that sister of yours."

"She is at that."

"How long ago did Abner, ah, pass?"

"A little more than two years." She scattered flour on the bread board. "Why?"

One shoulder lifted as he said, "Oh, no reason. Just askin'."

If she'd learned one thing, feeding multitudes of men at the diner, it was that they were too preoccupied with work and family to "just ask" anything. Anna pictured them together: Ella, tiny and energetic, beside the tall, barrel-chested man. If her sister ever decided to remove her black widow's garb, she could do worse than Matthew, who put in eight hours here and another eight helping to keep his brother's struggling farm afloat. A man like that would love and protect her fully, and no one deserved it more than Ella.

"What's the rule about grievin'?"

"I suppose that's a personal thing, something the husband or wife must decide for themselves if they lose a spouse."

"Tell me what to add to the stock, and I'll finish up your chicken soup."

Smiling to herself, Anna poured flour into a big glass bowl and dropped in cold butter cubes. *Changing the subject, eh, Matthew?*

"There's a recipe on the box on the shelf. It was my grandmother's."

He grabbed it, thumbed through the cards. "Fannie's *maem* or Elmer's?"

"*Daed*'s. And please don't be nervous. You've cooked up all sorts of delicious dishes. I'm sure the soup will be one of them."

While Anna cut the butter into the flour, Matthew added salt and pepper, diced onions and carrots, and cut chunks of baked chicken she'd prepped yesterday.

"I didn't know her as a girl. Did she go through an awkward stage, or has she always been pretty?"

Any doubts she'd had about his feelings disappeared with that question. Suppressing a snicker, she said, "Ella has been beautiful, inside-out, from the day she was born."

Grabbing the big stainless spoon from its hook above the stove, he said, "I remember Abner. He was a good man. Guess that's why she still mourns him." He dropped celery leaves into the pot, gave it a good stir. "Makes me wonder, though…"

Anna waited for him to complete his thought.

"…how much prettier she would look in green, like her eyes, or pink, or yellow, even."

Ella had been wearing black for so long that Anna couldn't picture her in another color. Would hearing that Matthew was interested inspire her to set aside her grief? How lovely would that be! With so little chance of marrying and having children of her own, Anna could live vicariously through her sister.

Anna poured cold water into the bowl, wondering when self-

The Blessings Jar

centeredness had become her dominant character trait. *Since you decided that your childish dream was more important than David's happiness.*

She kneaded the dough, rolled it out, and tamped it into a buttered pie pan, then spooned in the drained peaches and topped them with more flattened dough.

"What's wrong?"

She stopped crimping the crust. "Nothing, Matthew. Why?"

"You are pinching that dough so hard, I half expect it to yell 'ouch'!"

"If you thought that was something," she said, grasping a paring knife, "wait until you see this." Anna held it high, as if to stab the pie to death. When his eyes widened, she laughed—too long and too loud—and let the blade form a fanciful P in its center.

"Will you set the oven to 425 degrees?"

"Happy to," he said, and set the dial.

It would only take a short while to heat up. Then, in fifteen minutes, she'd reduce the heat to 375. The clock above the door said fifteen minutes before seven. By ten o'clock, Charlotte would have a hot-from-the-oven, almost homemade pie. That left plenty of time to mix up the pancake and waffle batter, start the breakfast biscuits, and fry up some sausage.

Fannie parked her wheelchair in the doorway between the kitchen and the dining room and jabbed a finger in the direction of the big pitcher on the counter. "Why did you mix up that batter already?"

Rather than remind her that letting it rest assured fluffier pancakes, Anna said, "I'd better get the coffee pots going. The truckers and construction workers will show up soon."

Her mother snorted. "When *I* ran the place, we opened at dawn, stayed open until dark."

Maybe that's why you were nearly bankrupt when I stepped in.

Let's All Eat would never make them rich, but the profits allowed Anna to pay off old debts, write paychecks—and give Matthew and Luke modest raises—and add to the diner's bank account. She'd expanded the menu, and using her own funds, purchased modern equipment and furnishings. Anna had also hired workmen to paint, replace flooring, and renovate the restrooms. The newly-paved parking lot and landscaped front entrance not only invited compliments

The Blessings Jar

from regulars, but attracted new diners, as well. So while the square footage hadn't increased, the number of meal orders had.

Although Anna had spent much of her life right here, washing dishes and waiting tables, she'd learned nothing about the business side of the restaurant. Despite that, she'd quickly adapted to her new administrative duties. At first, Elmer showered her with praise… until Fannie called them to task for their sins of vanity and pride. What a shame that her harsh, judgmental attitude compelled them to keep their joy a secret from her.

It hit her like a blast of icy wind: Secrets were at the root of hurt feelings, suspicions, and mistrust. Like thick fog that shrouded the mountains, hiding their beauty and majesty—and dangerous hairpin turns, deadly ice, and disabled vehicles—secrets were responsible for disappointment, broken hearts… and shattered dreams.

Anna interpreted everything that had happened today as the answer to prayer. The Almighty *did* want her to come clean with David, as soon as possible.

She slid the pie into the oven and set the timer for fifteen minutes. "Who would have thought pie could solve problems and ease minds?"

"Sorry," Matthew said, turning from the sink, "I couldn't hear you over the running water."

"Oh, nothing. Just talking to myself."

He chuckled. "The best way to guarantee someone is listening."

Anna headed for the dining room. "What are the chances my mother has wrapped the silverware in napkins and set the tables?"

Busy scrubbing potatoes, he hadn't heard her. Just as well. She'd sounded like an angry, bitter woman, even to herself. The additional character flaw would make it easier to talk to David, and easier to accept rejection when he wisely chose to further distance himself from her faults and flaws…

…and Anna, herself.

∼

He'd just finished stapling new mesh wire to the final enclosure gate when Cash scampered up beside him. "If I didn't know better," David said, patting the dog's head, "I'd say you can read my mind."

The pup answered with a whispery bark.

"Seems you've figured out that I'm finished for the day. Now I

The Blessings Jar

suppose you want to take a run."

Another whispery bark, and a smile, too. Then, ears perked, the pointer stared toward the vehicle crunching up the gravel drive. It resembled most cars in Pleasant Valley—plain, gray, four doors—and the closer it got, the louder Cash barked.

"Easy, boy. Could be a new customer."

Together, they walked toward the driveway's edge, and immediately saw that it wasn't a potential buyer. It was Anna, looking simultaneously cute and beautiful as she concentrated on keeping the car centered in the driveway. Long before Charity pointed her out, David had seen her, at the diner, across the church, at community gatherings. He'd been just twenty-two, and she a blushing, giggling fourteen-year-old... enough of an age gap that he'd felt guilty for so much as noticing her big green eyes and the earthy red curls, peeking from under her cap. She'd grown more beautiful with time, making him wish he could rewrite his past.

"Well, hello, Cash," she said, opening the driver's door. "Aren't you a pretty?"

The pointer peered up at David, as if asking permission to leave his side. And then, before David could give it, Cash moved close, tail wagging as she cooed and patted his head.

"Good to see you out of the diner for a change."

She swiveled on the seat and both feet hit the gravel at the same time. "It's good to *be* out of the diner."

He extended a hand to help her stand. At first, Anna seemed reluctant to take it, but when at last she put hers into it, David's heart pounded so hard that he worried she'd feel the pulsing in his fingertips.

"Considering your fear of birds, I'm surprised to see you here."

"This isn't my first visit to Red Oak Farm."

"It isn't?"

"Several times," she said, opening the rear door, "I've brought my mother to visit yours."

It was the first he'd heard about it.

Anna reached into the back seat. "Today, I'm here to deliver this."

David peeked under the blue-checkered kitchen towel. "A pie?"

"For your father's birthday. Your mother told mine it's to round out the celebration."

The Blessings Jar

It was the first he'd heard about that, too. Why hadn't his mother mentioned the party... or the visits?

"Did she give you a tour of the place?"

"Oh, goodness, no!" Her shoulders wiggled, like someone shaking off a chill.

"Ah, yes. Your fear of birds."

"Well, that, but mostly, I rarely had time. Once I got *Maem* and her wheelchair unloaded and situated, I mean."

"And then reloaded and resituated..."

"Something like that."

What would she say if he told her how much he'd always enjoyed her smiling, pink-cheeked face?

She'd say you're strange, he thought, and cleared his throat.

"Let's put this inside, and I'll show you around."

"I just came to drop off the pie and..." She bit her lower lip, then said, "I left poor Ella and Matthew alone at the diner."

Alone, with Fannie? But the real question was, what had she stopped herself from saying just now?

"It won't take long. I'll give you the speed tour." He started walking toward the house. "Who knows? Maybe afterward, your fear of birds will have vanished."

When he noticed that she had to half-run to keep up with his long strides, David slowed his pace, and as they crossed the space between her car and the porch, she whispered, "You should tell Charlotte that the peaches are not fresh."

"I doubt that will matter." He opened the door with the intention of placing the pie on the sideboard in the entry hall, but when she stepped in beside him, what choice did he have but to ask, "Coffee?"

Clutching her coat collar, she shook her head. "David, I, ah, there's something… I, um, I need…" She exhaled an exasperated sigh. "Is there somewhere—"

"Anna!" Charlotte exclaimed.

Anna looked as surprised as he felt. "*Maem*? I thought you and *Daed* were in Oakland, picking out your new clothes dryer."

She waved the comment away. "Oh, we decided to go later." Eyes narrowed, she said, "Have you had that talk with you-know-who?"

"No." And he wasn't looking forward to it, either. "But I will."

"When?"

The Blessings Jar

"Later."

"Today?"

He saw Anna glance at the banjo clock on the wall behind him. She wanted to leave, and he didn't want her to. Not just yet. Now it was his turn to exhale an exasperated sigh. Thankfully, his mother got the message. Hands clasped under her chin, she faced Anna.

"What—or should I say *who*—brings you here?"

Eyes wide, Anna pointed at the pie. "My mother said you asked me to bake it? For Robert's birthday?"

"Oh. Yes. That."

Why did she sound disappointed?

"I expect it'll be delicious, because everything you cook and bake is." Turning to David once more, she said, "Will you pay the dear girl, son?"

"My billfold is upstairs. I'll get it and—"

Anna grasped his forearm. "No need, really. It's a gift, from my mother to all of you."

"How *is* Fannie?"

Releasing him, she said, "All is well, and she said to tell you hello."

"I promised Anna a tour," David interrupted, "and she's on a tight schedule."

"A tour? Of the *farm*? But I thought—"

"If you see Isaac before I get back, ask him to check on that order for the DuVall company."

One hand pressed to the small of Anna's back, he led her outside before his mother could think of another stall tactic.

"Where would you like to start?"

"Much as I'd like to get over my fears, could we do it another day?"

"Sure. Of course." She started walking toward her car, and he followed. "I'm already looking forward to it."

Just then, Broze sped across the yard, wings up and chest puffed out, and yelping as though he'd entered a contest. The turkey startled her, and as Anna backpedaled away, she lost her footing. If David hadn't pulled her close, she would have landed on her keester. As she trembled in his arms, a strange new sensation washed over him. He wanted to protect her, from Broze, from long, hard hours at the diner,

The Blessings Jar

from her mother's sharp tongue.

"He's harmless," David assured.

Anna clung to him, and he held her tighter. "You have my word, he's as gentle as a lamb."

Despite her thick coat, he felt her heart, beating hard against his chest.

"His name is Broze."

Her eyebrows rose slightly. "Really?"

He returned her smile. "What. You think that's an odd name for a turkey?"

"It's an odd name, *period*."

"Want to pet him?"

"Mmm, that's okay."

"Want to watch *me* pet him, so you can see for yourself that he's as affectionate as a puppy?" David wanted her to say no, so he wouldn't have to turn her loose.

When she stayed put, he said, "Twice in the short time you've been here, you started to say something, but stopped yourself."

Anna stiffened and looked away.

"You want to say it, now?"

She shook her head. "I have to go." She took a step back, then another, and stopped when the turkey strutted close and rubbed his head on her calf.

"Is he *purring*?"

David chuckled. "Yep. So tell me, who's better at it, Broze, or your cat?"

"Mouser is louder, but…"

She sidestepped all the way to her car, and Broze sidestepped with her. Once she'd reached the vehicle, Anna pressed her backside against the driver's door. He couldn't stand to see her so afraid—and trying hard to hide it—so David hunkered down and held out his arms for Broze.

"Thank you," she said, and quickly got into the car. She rolled down the window. "Two new menu items tonight, in case you're planning on supper at the diner."

"Oh?" He scratched Broze's neck.

"Pot roast with all the trimmings, and breakfast, all day long."

"I'd better stay home tonight." *Considering that Maem planned a birthday dinner*.

"Yes. Right. Of course." She revved the engine.

"Anna?"

"David?"

As she buckled her seatbelt, he said, "When *will* you tell me?"

In place of an answer, she held his gaze for what felt like a full minute.

"Tell your father I said happy birthday."

CHAPTER 5

Ella threw open the door, looking happier than she had months. "I'm so glad you stopped by," she said, leading the way into the fitting room. "Come in so you can see the gown!"

Since leaving Red Oak Farm, Anna had felt on the verge of tears, but her sister's joy was contagious.

"There it is, and except for a few tucks here and there—the bride gained a few pounds—it's nearly finished."

Anna walked a circle around the dress form, inspecting layer upon layer of its gauzy white skirt. Ella had sewn white satin buttons to the long, lacy sleeves, and from the high-collared back to the wide, smocked waistband.

"Oh, Ella, it's stunning." Standing back, she said, "Remember that magazine we found in the recovery room after the accident?"

"Like it was yesterday. Page after page of glossy pictures of movie stars' gowns."

They'd sat side by side, oohing and ahhing over flouncy skirts, long, shimmering trains, and lacy veils. To that point, the only wedding dresses they'd seen had been light blue or pale gray... and Plain... so the pictures had inspired dreamy, whispered gasps. Ella's favorite had been Princess Grace's.

"Will your bride wear a see-through veil, like the princess's?"

Ella went to the rolling clothes rack against the wall and, carrying the headdress like a swaddled baby, presented it to Anna. Like the gown, its beauty was found in the simplicity of its soft white folds and hundreds of shimmering overcast stitches along the hem.

"The border alone must have taken hours and hours!"

"I burned some midnight oil on this one, that's for sure."

"I don't know what you're charging her, but this"—she gestured toward the dress—"this is worth twice the price."

"Thank you." Ella grabbed Anna's forearm. "Don't tell *Maem,* because she'd scold me for the sin of pride, but I'm quite pleased with the way this turned out."

How heartwarming it was to see pure joy instead of still-missing-

Abner sadness on Ella's face.

"I should let you finish up."

"Yes, and we both need to get back to work, too, but first, I need your input on something."

She led Anna to the kitchen, filled two mugs with coffee, and sat across from her at the table.

"I had to go back to the diner this morning." She rolled her eyes. "Left my mittens beside the cash register. And while I was there, Matthew called me up to the order window."

"What did he want?" Anna recalled the questions he'd asked earlier. Did they have something to do with Ella's jubilant mood?

"To see how long I intended to wear black."

"And you said…"

"That I really hadn't thought about it."

She seemed to have more to say, and Anna drew it out with, "But you have, haven't you?"

"That's just it. I'm not sure. Some women mourn for the rest of their lives. Others remarry quickly. As for me?" Ella shrugged. "I made promises on my wedding day."

The Blessings Jar

Anna was only too aware, because she'd echoed the words, mentally, trusting as she did that one day, she could say them to David: "*Do you both promise that you will come together with love, forbearance, and patience, live with each other, and not part from each other until God will separate you in death?*"

She reached across the table, blanketed Ella's hand with her own. "Your marriage was regrettably short, but both of you fulfilled your promises, to God and to each other." Pausing, Anna said, "Have you asked yourself what *He* might want for your future?"

Ella squeezed Anna's hand. "What a silly question. Who can know the mind of God?"

"No," she said softly, "I mean Abner. You're only twenty-five, with a long life ahead of you. Do you think he'd want you to spend it alone, pining away for him? Or would he want you to share it with someone who will love you, care for you, as he did?"

"You're right. I've given it a lot of thought and spent countless hours praying about it. So, when Matthew asked the question, I wondered... was it God's way of telling me it's time? Or wishful thinking? Because Anna, you have no idea how *lonely* I've been."

Anna knew a little about loneliness. The empty feelings had always made her feel embarrassed, because the Lord had richly blessed her with good health, sturdy shelter, plenty to eat, money enough to live comfortably, family and friends. Only an ungrateful brat would enjoy those gifts and still want more. Just one thing more. *David.*

Lifting her shoulders, Ella clasped her hands together. "Do you know what he said?" She leaned forward, and although they were alone in Ella's cozy kitchen, her sister whispered, "That he's a patient man, willing to wait until my grief has passed. That until that time, he wants to join me at gatherings."

How like her friend and hard-working employee to extend the hand of friendship as well as the promise of more.

"His kindness made me realize, I *am* ready to put away my widow's frock."

Anna stood, went around to Ella's side of the table, and gave her a sideways hug. "Oh, sister dear, you have no idea how happy this makes me!" There was only one thing that could make her happier. *David.* But this was neither the time nor place for such imaginings.

"You said yes, you'll attend socials together, I hope."

The Blessings Jar

"I did." She giggled like a schoolgirl. "I'm not so foolish as to think this small first step will lead to anything permanent. We barely know one another, Matthew and me, even though we've grown up in the same small community. It's possible that as we get better acquainted, we'll realize that we have nothing in common, or discover a bad habit, or a secret will be exposed that we just can't live with… until God separates us with death."

Secret. That awful *word* again. And like a coward, she'd walked away from the perfect chance to expose hers to David.

She thought about how safe, how secure she'd felt, standing in the protective circle of his arms, and the look of genuine concern that had drawn his almost-blond eyebrows together and turned down the corners of his mouth. How wonderful it would be, looking into those not-quite-green, not-quite-brown eyes, every day, for the rest of her life!

It would take strength like she'd never exerted to tell him what he deserved to hear: He was a good and decent man, regardless of what Anna had observed from her hiding place in the schoolhouse.

"Anna," Ella said, breaking into her thoughts, "if I didn't know better, I'd say you're about to burst into tears. What's wrong?"

Shaking her head, Anna summoned the self-control to say, "I'm just so happy for you." It was true, after all. It had been the right thing to say, as evidenced by the relief in Ella's eyes.

"It's a bit early to celebrate, but I appreciate your support. I've *always* appreciated you."

Anna chugged the now lukewarm coffee and put the mug into the sink. "Will I see you tonight?"

"Probably not. The wedding is next weekend, and I have to finish up the mother-of-the-bride and maid-of-honor dresses."

Just as well, Anna supposed, because tonight, she intended to write up a script of sorts to ensure she wouldn't shy away from the truth when she saw David again.

She'd pray, too, that once the secret was out in the open—at least between the two of them—he wouldn't shy away from *her*.

∽

The week passed slowly, in spite of regular visits to the diner. Yes, he'd enjoyed watching her race back and forth between tables, treating every patron like family. As always, the portions she'd delivered to him and Isaac had been bigger than most others, but it seemed she'd spent less time, chatting with them about everyday things like weather and the quickly turning calendar pages. He couldn't help but wonder if the difference was related to whatever she'd started to say—or ask—on pie delivery day.

Holding her in his arms stirred a yearning like none he'd ever felt and made him acutely aware of just how isolated he'd always been, even in a room filled with family and friends. Memory of those sweet moments caused dreams—of bringing her close, looking deep into those extraordinary green eyes, and basking in the light of her warm smile. All these years, he'd kept his feelings to himself. In his opinion, there was no other way to protect her from the truth about his past. If he could be sure she'd never find out…

Standing on her side of the counter, Anna refilled his mug. "Will you both want the usual this afternoon?"

"Cheeseburger. Fries. Cole slaw," Isaac answered, "and sweet iced tea." He turned to David. "You, too?"

"Yeah, I guess so."

"Back in few minutes with your orders," she said, and hurried off.

That's what was wrong today, David realized, a slightly more distant attitude, a little less friendliness in her eyes. He could blame the lunch rush… if it wasn't nearly three o'clock. Might fault Fannie's constant criticism… but so far, the woman hadn't uttered a negative word. It hurt and, having no way to explain why, made him feel foolish, too. From out of nowhere, his mother's reminder to talk with Josephs popped into his head. He liked to think he was a man of his word, a man who kept his promises.

"Anna," he called across the diner, and when she turned to face him, his heartbeat doubled. "Put a hold on my burger, will you please? I have to go. Just remembered something I have to do."

"Would you like a to-go order, instead?"

A glimmer of warmth sparked in her eyes. *It only takes a spark to start a fire…* Something to wish for? David grasped the wide-brimmed black hat that he'd hung from his knee as Isaac turned on his stool to face him.

"Is it something I can do?"

David gave his shoulder a brotherly squeeze. "No, friend. I need to handle this myself." On his feet now, he donned the hat, and noticed

The Blessings Jar

that Anna was watching him. Watching, as concern etched frown lines on her brow. Seeing it, his pulse quickened again. There was but one way to put a stop to the illogical reactions: Meet with her face to face, to see if she, too, had been hiding her feelings these many years.

Her tiny smile traveled the space between them, as if riding a nonexistent draft. A sign from God that she *did*? He turned to leave, thinking *a man can dream*.

As he drove back to Red Oak, David readied himself for the confrontation. He'd already stuffed an envelope with five thousand dollars, more than enough to tide the man over until he found work elsewhere. He'd taken the liberty of writing a letter of recommendation, too, and tucked it in with the cash. With any luck, the money would ease any hard feelings.

David unlocked his top desk drawer and removed the envelope, then walked quickly to the plant. As expected, he found Josephs in the break room, devouring a bologna sandwich. While it was customary for the men to alternate lunch times to make sure the operation continued running smoothly, none ate at this hour. And none ate alone.

"Hey, boss. How goes it?"

"It goes." Placing the envelope on the table, he sat across from the errant employee.

"Checking on production a day early, eh?"

"I need to discuss something with you."

"Whatever it is, I didn't do it." He threw back his head and cut loose with a loud, annoying guffaw.

Once he'd quieted down, David continued. "During my last inspection, I noticed that you left your position on the line. *Again*."

Lips taut and eyes narrowed, Josephs thundered, "Impossible! Who's telling you such things?"

David calmly repeated what he'd just said, adding, "When we talked six weeks ago, you made promises, *again*, and again, I took you at your word." He tapped the tabletop to emphasize each point: "Clock in and out on time." *Tap.* "No adjusting or modifying equipment." *Tap.* "No stepping away from the line without finding someone to stand in for you." *Tap.* "These are the rules every employee is expected to follow, myself included."

Josephs shoved his glasses higher on his nose, stroked his beard, and sat back in his chair. "I have stomach issues and need the restroom more than others."

David wanted to say, *"I don't believe it."* Instead, he said, "Last time, migraines were to blame. And the time before that, back strain."

The man's face reddened as he stared David down.

"You are a family man, so believe me, this decision didn't come easily." He slid the envelope forward until it touched the waxed paper under the man's food. "Full pay, through February, plus a letter of recommendation. That should tide you over until you find work elsewhere."

Josephs opened the envelope, removed the letter and read aloud:

"To Whom It May Concern:

During Michael Josephs' employment as a production associate at Red Oak Farm in Oakland, Maryland, he worked a total of 50 months, and proved himself to be articulate, enthusiastic, and self-motivated.

Feel free to direct questions to me at 301-333-1234.

Sincerely,
David Baden
Owner, Red Oak Farm"

Slowly and calmly, he refolded the letter and returned it to the envelope, then thumbed through the inch-thick stack of ten and twenty dollar bills.

"Must have taken all of a minute to write a letter that says nothing."

Actually, it had taken hours, because while David wanted no part of hindering future job opportunities, he hadn't wanted to lie either.

"But I like my job, so"—he shoved the envelope back to David—"thanks, but no thanks."

He'd expected shouting. Pacing. Maybe even tears. But this?

"As I said, it was a difficult decision, but it's final." For the second—and God willing, the last time—he pushed the envelope forward. David didn't want to mention his mother's complaints, but if the challenge continued, he would. "It's a fair severance package, Michael. Considering your work history and attitude, even you should be able to see that."

"What I *see* is a man who has succeeded, despite… everything."

David tensed and immediately pictured the semi dark schoolhouse.

The Blessings Jar

Martin Schwartz. Books hitting the floor as the deacon elbowed them from the teacher's desk…

Arms crossed over his chest, Josephs said, "You're not the only one."

CHAPTER 6

David padded away from the shower, and while toweling off, stood at the sink.

"You *look* like a guy who tossed and turned all night," he told his reflection.

And was it any wonder, with Josephs' last words still ringing in his head: *You're not the only one*.

He turned on the water, told himself not to jump to conclusions, that Josephs could have been referring to anything, from other employers who'd fired him to coworkers who thought he'd taken advantage of them.

The man's other statement, that David had succeeded "...*despite everything*" was even more disturbing.

Singly, the comments were innocuous enough, but together?

Together, they made his head spin and his gut churn.

The Blessings Jar

If he'd been more interested in information than avoiding Josephs' scathing glare, he might have some answers. But thirty-eight years of obedience to living Plain ran deep; New Order rules permitted modern conveniences—phones, electricity, plumbing, gas-powered vehicles that made the Amish more competitive in the business world—but confrontations of any kind had always been and would always be expressly forbidden. Josephs had been spoiling for a fight, and David had been angry enough—and afraid enough—to give it to him. When the dust settled, he might have walked away with answers, but at what cost?

Pitching the towel onto the hamper, he scrubbed both palms over his stubbled cheeks, then turned on the water and lathered his face. After slapping the razor back and forth across the strop, David scraped away his whiskers, watching as they swirled down the drain. How long would it take, he wondered, to grow a beard like his married friends Max and Phillip, like his father, and Elmer, and Bishop Fisher?

"Stupid question," he told the man in the mirror, "given that only married men have beards and you… aren't."

David dressed in black trousers and a blue denim shirt. At his mother's request, everyone left their boots near the back door, an especially good thing this morning, since he planned to slip out of the house before Ethan, Isaac, and his parents woke. Not even Pleasant Valley's farmers were up yet, but he knew one person who was ready to face whatever the day might throw her way…

Anna.

David couldn't predict how she'd react to an early-hours visitor, but he'd soon find out. He'd already wasted too much time—*years,* in fact—getting to know her from his side of the diner counter: She liked yellow better than blue. Daisies were her favorite flowers. Given a choice between salad and cake, she'd take cake, "with a generous coating of buttercream frosting."

Through everyday conversations, he'd learned that her copy of Jack London's *Adventure* was tattered and torn, thanks to multiple reads, that Romans 8:38–9 were her go-to Scripture verses, and that she disliked loud noises because "…there is music in silence."

Watching her interact with friends and neighbors and strangers showed him that God had blessed her with a generous and energetic

The Blessings Jar

spirit, limitless patience, and boundless devotion; for proof, one only needed to acknowledge what she'd willingly and uncomplainingly sacrificed to care for her parents.

When he'd asked how she could remain kind and tolerant in the face of Fannie's verbal attacks, she'd calmly replied, "…there but for the grace of God…"

Anna wasn't fond of bugs—or birds!—and the only time he'd only heard her use the word *hate* had been when Isaac told her he'd killed a black snake in one of the turkey pens.

She loved the Lord, babies and old people, dogs, even a cat that hadn't earned its name.

And David wanted her to love *him*.

That meant starting at the beginning, with an apology for the way he'd behaved all those years ago when her friend Charity asked if he'd noticed then-fourteen-year-old Anna, and now admitting that he'd *always* noticed her.

When he pulled into the Hertzlers' driveway, his headlights panned the side yard, where Anna was scattering feed for her chickens. *I was right: She's up and at 'em*, he thought, smiling.

As he parked, she shaded her eyes from the bright beams and recognizing his pickup, Anna smiled, too.

David exited the still-running truck, boots crunching over the frosty grass as he walked closer. "Are you always up this at this hour?"

"Of course. Haven't you heard? 'The early bird gets the worm.'"

Behind her, illuminated by the headlights, he noticed a section of bent chicken wire, and pointed it out. "Any missing hens lately?"

She turned, followed his gaze. "I noticed that break in the fencing just this morning. Along with bloody feathers." Meeting his eyes, Anna said, "Coyotes, you think?"

David nodded. "Probably. But a determined fox or raccoon can do serious damage, too."

Her shoulders slumped under the added weight of the news. This, *this* was just the kind of thing he wished he could protect her from.

"How many birds did the culprit get?"

"Culprit," she repeated, smiling. "Only you would choose such a word."

A blast of cold, damp air hit him square in the face, and he ducked

The Blessings Jar

deeper into his collar.

"There's snow in the forecast, and I for one am *not* looking forward to another blizzard-after-blizzard winter."

"The price of living in the mountains, I suppose," he said, and pocketed his hands.

"Let's talk inside, where it's warm."

Talk? It meant she'd sensed that he had something to tell her.

What he had to say could wait until the fencing was repaired.

"You go inside out of the cold, while take I care of that." He pointed at the twisted wire. "I know, I know," David said, a hand up to forestall her objection, "you're perfectly capable of doing it yourself, but it's what I do on an almost-daily basis, so I can do it faster." And very likely, the repair would last longer.

"You're sure?"

"I'm sure. Just show me where I can find some tools and supplies, and it'll be good as new in no time."

"All right, then." She started for the house, then stopped. "I'll probably have to leave for the diner before you're finished. Stop by and I'll make your favorite breakfast." She copied his gesture and held up a hand to add, "It's the least I can do."

He had to admit, waffles and home fries sounded mighty good.

"You'll find everything you need in the shed, including a big gas lantern that'll light up half the yard. That way, you won't need to run down your battery, leaving the headlights on."

"Thanks, Anna."

"No, thank *you*. Will I see you later?"

"Yes." *Definitely*. He thanked God for the extra time. *I'll make good use of it*. He prayed to ask Him to guide his words, make Anna receptive to them, and bolster his courage… in case the ugly truth gave her reason to reject him.

She went one way and he went the other, each with their own duties and agendas. One day soon, David hoped they'd walk together, side by side, toward a singular goal: Love and family.

∽

Anna couldn't remember a more difficult day at the diner.

Gale force winds loosened bolts that held the upblast ventilator to the roof, and while Matthew was up there tightening things, the blasts

The Blessings Jar

nearly blew him down to the parking lot. Fannie, angry because Elmer wouldn't move from one side of their special table to the other, pitched a fit... and crashed into a man paying his bill. Anna offered free meals as an apology, and although his refusal had been gracious, she didn't expect to see him again. Two diners knocked over full glasses of sweet tea, two more elbowed food-covered plates from their tables, and a foursome sneaked out without paying their tab. Luke called from the ER to report that a horse had tromped on his foot, and the truck carrying her long-awaited delivery of soft drink cannisters had broken down on the highway, all during the lunch rush.

Laundry and ironing waited for her at home, but by two o'clock, Anna had already decided it could wait. She'd lock up, take her parents' home, and spend the evening reading beside the fire.

During the short drive home, Fannie had been uncharacteristically quiet. Which should Anna credit for the peace and quiet... the embarrassing scene at the diner, or Mable Troyer's loud reaction to it: "I feel bad about what happened to her, but honestly, that woman is meaner than Jubal Quinn's bull, Goliath." Anna had to give her father credit for not rubbing *Maem*'s nose in it. How good it was to listen, instead, to his comments about odd-colored cars, truck traffic, and the quickly falling leaves.

She'd fixed them a simple snack of cheese, crackers, and apple slices, and by nine o'clock, they'd turned out the lights. Fannie's steady snores told her it was safe to cozy-up with her book.

It was going on ten when headlight beams, turning into the drive, slid across the ceiling. "Who could that be?" she said to Mouser. The cat was none too happy when Anna got to her knees on the sofa and parted the curtains to peer outside.

David, twice in one day?

She raced to open the door, because even quiet rapping might wake her father.

He looked tired—and no wonder, considering how early he'd stopped by this morning—but not even exhaustion dimmed his friendly smile.

"I saw your light," he said, stepping into the kitchen. "Hope it's all right that I stopped by so late."

The Blessings Jar

"Early, late, you're always welcome." She spoke softly. "Coffee? And I made apple cobbler. It's still warm…"

"So that's what smells so good." He glanced at the baking pan. "But I'd better not. Coffee sounds good, though."

"Hang up your coat and hat," she whispered, "and warm yourself by the fire while I heat up the coffee."

I'm warm enough right here, he thought.

David hung his things beside hers near the door, then looked around. Clean. Tidy. Organized. Just like the diner. Just like *Anna*. If he hadn't heard about the renovations that made the house wheelchair accessible, he would have assumed it always looked this way.

Moving to the woodstove, he sat on his heels and opened the heavy iron door, then eased in a few logs.

"I hope I'm not making too much noise."

"You aren't." Anna poured coffee into two mugs.

"Your parents are sound sleepers?"

"My mother is," she said, putting the mugs on the table, "but *Daed* has a lot of trouble sleeping."

Sitting beside her, he nodded. "Because he's in pain?"

"Not the physical kind. He remembers how things were before the accident, when he was strong and active, and completely independent." She wrapped both hands around her mug. "I sometimes wonder if he'll ever adjust to his... condition."

"Understandable," he admitted. "I've asked myself how I'd fare under similar circumstances."

"That doesn't surprise me."

He took a sip of coffee. "You really don't mind that I stopped by so late? Uninvited?"

"Not at all. In fact, I'm glad you're here."

A simple statement, really, one Anna might have made to a diner patron she hadn't seen in a while or a church-goer who'd missed several Sunday services. It probably wasn't the best idea to attach special meaning to it, and yet, that's exactly what he did.

Anna continued with, "I need to say something... something I should have said a long, long time ago."

The music in her voice had dimmed. Was this *something* connected to what she'd tried to tell him the other day?

"But first, I want you to know that I care about you, about what happens to you, what's good for you. Always have, always will."

"I feel the same way about you."

She gazed deep into his eyes, then turned away. "Please don't look at me that way."

"What way?"

Anna tilted the mug left, then right. "As if you think I'm a better person than I am. Because believe me, I have flaws. Big ones, and a lot of them."

"You'd have a hard time convincing anyone in Pleasant Valley of that. Me, in particular."

She held his gaze for a long, silent moment, then said, "David, stop."

"Why? You know that old saying, 'Actions speak louder than words'?"

Now Anna stared into her mug.

"*If* you have a flaw, it's that you undervalue yourself. Everything I've seen and heard proves that you *are* a good person."

Anna sat sideways on the chair seat, eyes flashing, jaw and fists clenched, and he had no idea why she was so angry.

His confusion ended when she ground out, "I know what happened to you. I've known for *years*, but instead of helping you understand that there wasn't a thing you could have done to prevent it, this so-called good person took the coward's way out, and let you wall yourself off, from happiness, from…" She got to her feet so quickly that if he hadn't caught the chair, it would have clattered to the floor.

David hated seeing her upset.

But wait…

Had she actually said, *I know what happened to you.*"? It was eerily similar to Michael Josephs' taunt: "…*a man who succeeded, despite everything.*"

The two couldn't possibly be connected…

…could they?

And if there was a connection, how? And *why*?

It wasn't likely Deacon Schwartz talked, not even to Bishop Fisher. But if he had, could Josephs or Anna have listened in on the confession?

Overwhelmed, David stood and shoved both chairs under the table, then carried their mugs to the sink.

The Blessings Jar

"The chicken coop is fine now."

There were tears in her eyes when she said, "Thank you, David."

"I put the tools back where I found them."

His legs felt heavy, wooden, yet somehow, they carried him to the door, and he left without saying thanks for the coffee…

…without saying goodbye.

CHAPTER 7

David got up off his knees with a clear understanding of what he had to do.

"Ethan," he said, entering the Red Oak office, "I have an errand to run, so you're the go-to guy this morning."

As a kid, David's younger brother hadn't exactly exhibited leadership qualities. In fact, he'd been in trouble more often than not. But as he matured, Ethan made no secret of his desire to shoulder more business responsibility, and he proved his worth time and again.

"Something I can do, instead?"

"I'm afraid this is personal, and something I need to do myself. But thanks for the offer."

"Well, God go with you, brother."

Nodding, David left, and as he crossed the parking lot, admitted that as a boy, he'd caused his parents far more trouble and heartache

The Blessings Jar

than Ethan ever had. Small for his age, he'd convinced himself that bold-faced defiance would make him seem bigger, stronger, and in control of his world: Ditching school. Back-talking those in authority. Hitchhiking to town—without permission—and collecting dozens of tickets for loitering, littering, leaving soap-written messages on car windshields. Skipping services to go fishing. And when called on the carpet to explain the audacious actions, he'd blamed others, or lied, or both.

In an attempt to get him back in line, the Badens had tried everything from lectures to spankings to revoking privileges, all to no avail. In a last-ditch effort to "straighten him out," they went to the bishop, who recommended one-on-one Bible studies with Deacon Martin Schwartz. Two times a week, man and boy met, alone in the schoolhouse.

By the end of that first session, David saw that rebellion had branded him untrustworthy, incorrigible, a habitual liar… traits that became weapons in Schwartz's arsenal, weapons he'd put into use, twice weekly, for three agonizing years.

It was a thirty-minute drive from the heart of Pleasant Valley to the

Schwartz's house. Halfway there, it seemed to David that he'd already been on the road twice that long. A normal reaction, he thought, to doing something exceedingly difficult.

As he made the turn from Route 219 to 560 South, David's fingers began to ache. And no wonder, the way he'd been squeezing the steering wheel.

A year or so ago, Micah Fisher stopped by the Red Oak office, invited David to step outside, and walk with him. "You should know that Schwartz has cancer," the bishop had said. "He is dying, and needs your forgiveness to go in peace to his Maker."

Despite everything, he'd never wished ill upon the man. In fact, David had worked hard to avoid him, so hard that it sometimes felt like a part-time job. It required missing church services and community gatherings, which hadn't set well with his parents, especially since he couldn't tell them *why*. He eased his conscience by reminding himself that he'd also worked hard to make amends for the troubles he'd caused. And thanks to many hours in prayer about the matter, David believed God knew his heart, and understood. And that was good enough for him.

The Blessings Jar

A simple black-on-white sign came into view, starting a tremor that traveled from the pit of his stomach to his fingertips:

SCHWARTZ BEE FARM
Honey, Beeswax, Candles, Soap

David slowed to make the turn onto the winding, narrow, dirt road and pictured the honey-filled Mason jar his mother had purchased at last year's fall harvest. She'd bought candles and a bar of soap, too. It had taken months to teach himself not to notice the nightmarish reminders, but even after all this time, mental images of them had the power to raise the hair on the back of his neck.

"Lord," he muttered, parking near the house, "give me strength."

Schwartz's wife stood on the porch, hugging herself to fend off the chilly wind.

"I heard your truck," she said as he walked closer. "Martin hoped you would stop by."

As a young teen, David had been half her height and weight. Today, he towered over her. The years had not been kind to Polly Schwartz, as evidenced by hunched shoulders and thin bones. He had no proof she'd been aware of her husband's extracurricular activities, but based solely on appearances...

"Bishop Fisher tells me he's ill?"

"It is not like Micah to sugarcoat things. Martin is *dying*." One withered hand gestured toward the stairs. "First room on the right. I will bring tea."

"I appreciate the offer," David said, "but I'm not staying long."

She answered with an indifferent shrug and shuffled toward the kitchen.

Every other step creaked under his weight—another ominous reminder of the past—so he wasted no time climbing to the top. The thick maple door was slightly ajar. He raised a hand to knock, but snatched back his hand. Unexpectedly, his mouth went dry. What was he afraid of?

"David... ?"

The voice, like Polly's, was shaky and thin. He gave the door a push, and it swung slowly open with a high-pitched squeal.

Schwartz, propped up by thick pillows, waved him in.

"Bless you, boy, for coming."

The Blessings Jar

The big, brawny man whose authoritative baritone could silence even the most raucous crowd now more closely resembled the *Englischers*' bony Halloween decorations. His hair, sparse and white, stood out in all directions above bushy eyebrows. If not for the dull, staring eyes, it would have been hard to tell where he began and the pillowcases ended.

"Pull up a chair. Sit beside me. I have much to say and not much time to say it."

Did he sense that as a boy, he'd wanted little more than to see proof of some sort that the man was paying for his sins? If not for Romans 12:19, David might still be carrying the heavy burden of vengeance in his heart. Relaxing tightly-clenched fists, he said, "Sorry to hear about your illness."

He grimaced. Unable to believe it possible for David to show compassion?

"Your parents and brother are well, and Isaac?"

"All are well."

Schwartz sipped from the tumbler on his bed tray.

"And Anna, still caring for Elmer and Fannie?"

Why would he ask such a thing, unless he'd been watching, and knew that she'd filled every empty space in his heart, and helped him begin to forget—

He raised a skeletal hand, aimed a crooked forefinger in David's direction. "You would be wise to invite her into your life. She is a good woman."

David wanted to shout, *"After what you did, no good woman will want me!"*

"I regret my actions, David, and have asked God's pardon." Eyes closed and lower lip quivering, he said, "Very soon now, I will learn whether or not He has given it, but for now, I humbly ask your forgiveness."

After deciding to come here, David had made up his mind: If he couldn't tell the truth, he wouldn't speak at all. So he sat, elbows on knees, staring at the pistil and petals of the pink magnolia, woven into the rug beneath his boots. The flower blurred as he searched his soul: Could he fulfill Schwartz's request… without lying?

Nearly every book in the Bible referenced forgiveness, but one verse stood out: *"If you hold anything against anyone, forgive them, so that your Father in heaven may forgive you."*

He looked up, into the rheumy blue eyes of the gnarled old man whose repeated threats—"*If you tell, who will they believe? A boy who lies, or a man of God?*"—had guaranteed his protection, and chained David to years of shame and feelings of unworthiness.

"*Invite her into your life*," Schwartz had said. David might have laughed… if her words hadn't cut so deeply. Then a truth came to mind. Anna had prefaced her outburst with a tender admission: She cared about him; always had, always would.

The chains fell away, and the ache in his heart eased. Much as he hated to give Schwartz credit for anything good, the man had been right. Anna was as good as they came. All these years, she'd known. She'd known, and yet treated him with kindness and affection.

He got to his feet, ran a hand through his hair, and remembered that he'd promised to speak only the truth today.

"You are forgiven."

Schwartz closed his eyes and expelled a long, shaky sigh. "Bless you, boy. Bless you."

"Thank you," Polly said.

The suddenness of her voice startled him. How long had she been standing just outside her husband's door?

"You have given us the gift of peace."

As he drove away, he looked into the rearview mirror and watched as the Schwartz house, the beehives, the dusty, meandering road slipped into the distance... into the past.

Work, family, friends, and God had always been enough for him. But now he needed answers: Had Anna treated him well out of pity, or because she truly cared for him?

He risked another glance into the rearview, saw the glorious colors of the setting sun.

And if he invited her into his life, would she say yes?

It was nearly closing time, so David wasn't surprised to see just Ella's car and the wheelchair accessible van in the normally crowded parking lot. The red neon *Let's All Eat* sign was still lit, so he went inside, removed his hat and placed it on the front counter.

No one noticed him. A blessing in disguise, he thought, leaning an

The Blessings Jar

elbow beside the cash register. Now he'd have time to think and screw up the courage to ask Anna to talk with him later.

Elmer and Ella were nowhere in sight, so they must have been in back, wrapping silverware or filling condiment containers. Matthew or Luke had left for the day. Although he couldn't see Anna or Fannie, David heard their voices, just on the other side of the service counter: "I have had just about enough of your moping," Fannie said. "Tell me what put you in this foul mood, or I declare—"

"All right, I'll tell you, if only to stop the constant questions."

Anna sounded agitated, and who could blame her. Fannie could annoy the peaceful dove.

"I said some things to David the other night. Horrible, hateful things that he'll never forget… that he'll never forgive me for."

"Not *that,* I hope! Oh, Anna. You were to keep it to yourself, forever. Whatever made you tell him?"

"He deserved to hear that it wasn't his fault, that he isn't tainted by what the deacon did."

"It seems blasphemous to call him that."

She then launched into a dissertation:

The half dozen men, chosen by fellow parishioners, were none too pleased about the nominations. And neither were their wives, who wept openly, each aware that her husband might be chosen as the next servant to the community. The duties included collecting alms for the poor, assisting the bishop in matters of discipline, and publishing the names of couples who were to be married. He would never preach in the church. Instead, he performed all physical labor. The job, according to Fannie, was the most time consuming and thankless job in the church…

"…so is it any wonder that no man truly *wants* to the position. But when Martin's name was called," she continued, "Polly fainted, and the congregation burst into tears. Other men in his position wept, but not Martin. Martin looked pleased." She harrumphed again. "Now we know why: Easy pickins among the youngsters for his wicked perversions!"

Hearing it put so bluntly made David cringe. Thankfully, Anna steered the conversation to Thanksgiving, which wasn't far off.

"That reminds me," Fannie said. "Charlotte and I have decided to share the meal this year. All totaled, there will be nine at the table,

The Blessings Jar

and since our kitchen is larger, I offered it."

Silence.

"You should add *that* to your blessings jar. What is more wondrous than the blending of good friends on such an important day?"

He'd heard a few things about the vessel that held her hopes and dreams and—how had she put it, talking to Ella?—"...*things to thank God for.*"

"I have not looked forward to a holiday since the accident. Sharing a meal with the Badens will give us *all* something to look forward to, don't you think?

Again, silence.

Having spent so much time in her presence, David thought he knew what was going on.

When Anna admitted to her mother that she'd "said some things," he'd heard sincere regret in her voice. If only he could tell her, right here and now, that there was nothing to forgive.

Frustrated, he slapped a palm to the back of his neck, bumping his hat and overturning the basket of foil-wrapped mints on the counter as Anna peeked around the pass-through window.

"David..."

"Hi," he said, picking up spilled mints. "Am I too late for pie and coffee?"

CHAPTER 8

David didn't look angry. Maybe he really had stopped by for pie and coffee.

First thing in the morning, she'd drag the stepladder to the door and find out why the bells above the door hadn't signaled his entrance.

Right now, though, Anna wanted to thank him for fixing the chicken coop. For repairing the back gate and nailing down the loose boards on the front porch steps, fixing the wobbly railing, and oiling the screen door. But she still felt awful about what she'd said; if she could trust herself not to blubber like a baby, she'd tell him that he'd saved her hours of back-breaking, splinter-inducing work.

More worrisome than that, how long had he been here, and how much had he overheard? Enough to share her newly-formed opinion… that her mother's advice had been self-motivated, protecting her from the judgment of those who might judge her for raising a daughter who'd sneak into the schoolhouse for a book that wasn't hers.

Anna's guilt had doubled, listening as her mother described nomination procedures. How many other troubled youngsters had Schwartz taken advantage of because of the mother-daughter agreed-upon silence?

"It is closing time," Fannie said. "We have—"

"I've already cleaned the coffee maker," Anna interrupted, "and we were just about to go home. You're welcome to follow us, and if you can wait until I get *Maem* and *Daed* settled for the night, I'll make your favorite…"

A slanted grin lit his face.

"…to thank you for everything you did the other day."

"No thanks necessary. I was happy to help." He shifted his weight from one big-booted foot to the other and put on his hat. "I need to stop at the house first, check on a few things." Forefinger touching the black felt brim, he said, "See you soon."

The instant the door closed behind him, Fannie wheeled her chair around and faced Anna.

The Blessings Jar

"You cannot do this," she said. "He is... he is *damaged*." Rolling closer, she added, "You are way past marrying age, anyway, so why bother with—"

"Fannie!" Elmer shouted. "Stop it. Stop it this minute!"

It wasn't like her father to lose his temper. She watched him move his wheelchair closer to Fannie's.

Leaning forward, he said through clenched teeth, "Have you lost your mind? That is no way to talk to your *tochter*. Any man would be blessed to be part of Anna's life."

"I only want what is best for her, and David Baden is *not*."

Elmer thumped his chair's arm. "What happened was not his fault. Surely you know that!"

Anna knuckled the tears from her eyes. "*Daed,* you... you *know*?"

Fannie grunted. "Of course he knows. There can be no secrets between husband and wife."

If there had been any doubts about the real reason behind her mother's original advice—and she'd wondered about that, often—they died with that statement. Should she blame fatigue, sadness, or anger for the tears that stung her eyes?

She'd have to pray, long and hard, for the strength to obey the Fifth Commandment, which instructs believers to honor their parents… whether or not they deserve it.

∽

He'd heard the "deer in headlights" cliché before, but until Anna saw him near the diner's door, he hadn't fully understood its meaning. She'd looked astonished, afraid, ashamed, all rolled into one, and David could almost read her mind: *When did he arrive, and how much did he hear?*

Seeing her discomfort had made him feel bad, made him question his decision to remain quiet, and continue eavesdropping on the discussion between her and her mother. Standing still hadn't been easy, especially after hearing that Fannie was responsible for Anna's silence.

After leaving the diner, David had driven home, went straight up to his room, and spent an hour on his knees, seeking God's guidance: Visit Anna tonight… or avoid her, starting now?

His thoughts turned to the friendly banter, the silly puns, the comfortable conversations they'd shared at *Let's All Eat*. Lately, though he couldn't explain why, exactly, David had felt closer to her than ever before. Closer, and more able to imagine what life might be like with her at his side, instead of separated by the diner counter. Imagining it *without* her caused an ache so deep and wide that he put the question straight out of his mind and wasted no time getting to her house.

When he arrived, Anna opened the door wide. "I hope it isn't too late."

In place of an answer, she shook her head, loosening a curl from her bun. The minute he stepped inside, he noticed that her long dark lashes were spiky and damp, her green eyes puffy and red-rimmed. What awful thing had her mother said *this time*, he wondered, to make Anna cry?

"Coffee?"

"I'd better not. I've had my quota for the day."

"Tea, then. You'll need *some*thing to wash down the apple cobbler."

David removed his hat and coat, and hung them on an empty hook in the entryway as she quietly closed the door.

"Your mother and father are asleep?"

She adjusted the fire under the tea kettle. "I haven't heard a peep for half an hour or more, so I think so."

Good, David thought, watching her drop tea bags into earthenware mugs, because after what he'd overheard earlier, Fannie was the last person he wanted to see.

Through the woodstove's glass door, he noticed the fading glow of coals. Whenever possible, Ella helped care for Elmer and Fannie, but running the diner and maintenance of the house, inside and out, fell to Anna. Noah Briskey delivered firewood, but it was up to her to haul it inside and keep the home fires burning. David didn't know how she did it, all without complaint.

Down on one knee, he stirred the embers as her cat sauntered up and loosed a sound that was somewhat like a meow. "Well, hello, Mouser," he said, and grabbed the bellows to fan the flames and added two logs. Satisfied that she'd secured his notice, Mouser made her way to Anna, and walked figure eights around her shoes.

"Silly thing," she said. "Are you trying to get stepped on?" She glanced at him. "Thank you, David."

"Happy to do it," he said, standing. "I only wish I could do more."

She carried two plates to the table. "You couldn't possibly do more."

She'd referred, he knew, to the odd jobs he'd so recently performed at the Hertzlers' house.

"That cobbler smells delicious."

"It's hot from the oven. I needed something to occupy my mind," she said, reaching into the freezer, "once I'd settled them in for the night." She placed a carton on the table and removed its lid. "Soon as I pour our tea, I'll serve it up."

He opened and closed a few drawers, and after finding the one where she'd stored flatware, helped himself to one large spoon and two smaller ones, and proceeded to top their bowls with vanilla ice cream.

Anna delivered the tea and sat down. "Thank you," she said again.

"See?" he teased. "I *can* do more."

"It's very kind—and very typical—of you to offer. But you have more than enough on your shoulders already."

"Apples and oranges," he countered. "Plus, I have help. Ethan, Isaac, my parents, all the men who work at the plant." Elbows resting on the table's edge, he said, "You have no one."

"Yes, I do! I have Ella, Luke and Matthew, even *Maem* and *Daed* help when and how they're able."

No comparison, he thought.

"I'm sorry, David. So sorry, for… for everything."

David didn't want to relive the scene from the other night and didn't want to put her through it, either, so instead of asking why, he covered her hand with his own.

"Anna Hertzler," he said, "you have nothing to apologize for."

She stared at their hands, then said, "May I ask you a question?"

"I suppose…"

"What work were you forced to postpone to help me out the other day? Because I'm happy to help you catch up. It's the least I can do."

Word for word what she'd said in the diner a short time ago. Then, he'd shrugged it off as one of many things people say in passing. Now, he realized that for Anna, the statement was heartfelt.

"Oh, just routine stuff."

"Such as?"

"Putting clean bedding in the turkey pens, scrubbing food and water dispensers, checking the temperature in the brooding house." He gave her hand an affectionate squeeze. "Nothing that couldn't wait."

The ice cream had formed a white puddle around his cobbler. She'd noticed it, too. He'd pick up his spoon and empty the bowl... if it didn't require letting go of her hand.

"May I ask *you* a question?"

"I suppose..." she said.

"Can you describe your typical day?"

Anna laughed, and the sound of it traveled through him, raising the memory of the time he'd stupidly tried to repair the cord on his mother's favorite lamp... without first unplugging it. He'd been eleven or twelve at the time, but clearly remembered the sizzling jolt.

"I can, but I won't. The list is so boring, it'll put you straight to sleep."

How could he explain that nothing about her bored him?

He let go of her hand and dipped into the cobbler. "Well, if I doze off, don't wake me." *Because I'll be dreaming of you... of us...*

"How about this: I'll recite the list *for* you."

She laughed again, and the music purled over him like warm rainwater.

"You're up by four," David began, "after feeding Mouser, over there, you fix something to tide your parents over until they can have a proper meal at the diner." He leaned a little closer. "Then you drive over to the diner to get things ready for your customers. Coffee. Bacon and sausage. Checking to make sure the dining room is tidy and the rest rooms are clean. Then it's back to the house, where you gather up everything they'll need for the day... medications, sweaters, change of clothes... And after helping them into the van, you're off again. And after settling them in at the diner..."

A peculiar little smile lifted one corner of her mouth.

"What?"

"If I didn't know how busy you are in the early-morning hours, I'd say you've been peeking into the windows, watching me." She threw back her head and laughed, then clamped a hand over her mouth to silence herself.

"Yeah, stop that," he said. "You don't want to wake..." He looked left, right, then faked a shiver. "...*Fannie*..."

"Would you like more cobbler?" she asked, pointing at his empty bowl.

David hadn't realized he'd eaten it all. "Guess it's true what they say."

"Who?"

"The sages."

"What do they say?"

"That time flies while you're having fun."

Both perfectly arched eyebrows rose, and her eyes widened.

"Is it so hard to believe I enjoy spending time with you?"

"No. Well. I just..." She hid behind her hands, but only for a moment. "My cowardice caused you pain. So many years of loneliness."

He took her hand again. "You're anything—"

A loud thud, shattering glass, and Fannie's high-pitched wail stopped him, mid-sentence.

Before he could get to his feet, Anna had darted from the room.

He followed, and it didn't take long to figure out what had happened: Somehow, her mother had upended the night table, breaking a lamp, a mug, and a cookie plate. Milk had splattered across the wall and onto the cracked cookies scattered across the braided rug.

"*Maem*," Anna said, sliding an arm across Fannie's shoulders, "are you all right?"

"Are you blind? I am soaked to the skin and surrounded by a mess. Of course I am not all right!"

"How can I help?" David asked from the doorway.

Until now, Fannie hadn't noticed him. "What is *he* doing here?" she demanded.

"I fixed a few things around here the other day and wanted to give Anna a few tips to prevent problems in the future." And he would have, if not for Fannie's accident.

She looked at Anna. "I do not want him here, watching while you clean up. Send him home. Send him away!"

Elmer levered himself up onto one elbow. "Thank you, David. And I apologize for my wife's harsh words. She does not handle pain well at all."

Another old saying came to mind: "*I'm so embarrassed, I wish the floor could open up and swallow me.*" Anna looked that way right now. Something told him he'd help her more by leaving than by helping her clean up.

"I'll go," he told her. "Thanks for the tea and cobbler."

"I would send you home with some, but…" She looked at the bed, at the floor and wall, at the upturned nightstand.

"It's all right. See you tomorrow."

David made his way to the back door, praying as he went that Fannie wouldn't give Anna a hard time as she put things back in order, that when the work was done, Anna could quickly put it out of her mind, and get a much-needed good night's sleep.

As he passed through the kitchen, David saw their mugs and bowls, right where they'd left them on the table. The last thing she needed was to find this mess when she'd finished cleaning up Fannie's.

He immersed the dishes in hot, soapy water. Covered the leftover cobbler. Centered the salt and pepper shaker and napkin holder on the blue and white checked tablecloth. And after tossing the sodden teabags into the trash, he bundled up the bag, thinking to stuff it into the trash receptacle on his way to the truck.

Mouser walked another figure-eight yet, this time around David's boots. He scanned the kitchen, and seeing two ceramic bowls near the pantry, said, "Show me where Anna keeps your vittles, and I'll fill 'em up."

Round eyes—eyes almost the same shade of green as Anna's—met his, then flicked left.

"In there?"

The cat meowed.

Sure enough, he saw a ceramic canister labeled MOUSER on the shelf. Tucking it under one arm, he carried it across the room and dumped a scoopful of its contents into the bowl. Now, with her bowls full of food and water, he returned the container to the pantry.

David was buttoning his jacket when Mouser meowed, as if to say goodbye. Or thanks.

"Tell Anna to sleep well," he said, closing the door. *And that I love her…*

CHAPTER 9

David hadn't seen her in nearly two weeks, save a few meals here and there at the diner.

Business had always been steady, but these weeks before Thanksgiving had been busier than at any time of year, including Christmas.

Between filling current orders from grocery stores, restaurants, and frozen foods distributors, Red Oak crews were working double shifts to meet customer demands for fresh turkeys.

From what little he'd seen, things had picked up at the diner, too. Thanks to its location on the main highway—and being one of a handful of eateries along the Seneca Trail—*Let's All Eat* had become a popular stop, especially during the annual fall festival. Anna's long days had always been full, but these days, the word was an understatement.

Which probably explained why her wood pile was nearly depleted.

With the acceptance of New Order ways, many Pleasant Valley business owners utilized electric machinery, gas-powered vehicles, telephones, and computers for work, and most had installed them in their homes, too. Modern furnaces, however, were the exception rather than the rule. Fireplaces and woodstoves provided heat, even though the coldest winters. And the other night, as he'd stuffed garbage into the Hertzlers' trash can, he'd noticed that their firewood supply was dangerously low. With Anna's schedule, she'd probably forgotten to order more. So David called his best friend, Noah Briskey, owner of a generations-old logging company, to deliver a cord.

"'Bout time you got here," he said when the delivery truck rolled up.

Laughing, Noah said, "Yeah, I missed you, too, Brother Baden."

They spent the next half hour laughing as they unloaded, then stacked the logs between the back porch and the tool shed.

Admiring their work, Noah said, "Now that right there is just about the tidiest wood pile I've ever seen. Good choice, putting it a hop, skip, and a jump from the back door, close enough for a short walk to grab an armload, far enough to stop nesting bees from pestering the family. Anna will appreciate that when she fetches eggs."

David's thoughts, exactly. "Meet me at my office, and we'll settle up. Might even be a cup of coffee in it for you."

The men spent the next half hour reminiscing about foolhardy stunts they'd pulled as boys, and how if one got caught making mischief, the other would cover for him. Between stories, Noah talked about his wife and the house he hoped to finish before their first child arrived in the spring.

"How's Ella?" Noah asked. "Is she getting by on that little bit of money I send her every month?"

"She's doing all right, and so is her business." Cash's toenails click-clacked across the wood floor, and he flopped down near David's feet. "You can stop sending money. You'll need it soon, for that baby of yours."

"I don't know. What happened to Abner... I'll always feel responsible for that."

"He was a logger, Noah. It's dangerous work, and he knew that when he signed on with you."

"Yeah, well…"

"I know something that might change your mind."

"Yeah? What."

"I have it on good authority that Matthew is interested in her."

That brightened Noah's mood. "Matthew Zook?"

"One and the same."

"Well, I'll be." He nodded. "That is good news. For both of them."

"Yes, a good match. If he ever screws up the courage to tell her how he feels."

If you screwed up the courage, you might just—

"Speaking of good matches, how is Anna?"

"She's fine."

"C'mon, friend, 'fess up. Any news you want to share with your old friend?" He gave David a brotherly punch to the shoulder.

"No; why would there be?"

"Because when money got tight, you moved your folks and your brother into your house—a mother who's a fair to middlin' cook—yet more than half the time, you take your meals at the diner. You're sweet on her. Why else would you do that?"

He could remind Noah that Charlotte *wasn't* a fair to middlin' cook. Or he could say, "Sometimes, a man just needs a change of scenery." And oh, what lovely scenery it was!

~

Ella stood, hands on hips, inspecting their parents' room. "I don't know how you do it."

"One day at a time and a *lot* of prayer." Anna had replaced their mother's broken lamp with the one from her own bedside table and now straightened the plain ecru shade.

"Please tell me she didn't throw David out of the house."

"Let's just say she made it clear that he should leave." *But if I'd needed him, he would have stayed.*

"*Daed* told me about all the repairs David made around here." On the heels of a tiny sigh, Ella said, "He's such a good man."

"Yes. Yes, he is." Anna inspected the room and, satisfied that she'd cleared the last of Fannie's mishap, adjusted the pillow. Dishwater-roughened skin and calluses rasped across the crisp white cotton, and she jerked back her hand… the hand that he'd cradled in his own. If he'd noticed the coarseness, he showed no sign of it. But then, he seemed blind to all of her flaws.

"Don't get me wrong, I understand that she lashes out because she's angry and frustrated. It can't be easy for a woman who stayed busy from dawn till dark to sit in a chair, to need help with so many things. But really Anna, it's been *two years!* Why hasn't she adjusted by now?"

Anna took Ella's hand, led her from the room. "I have found that if I ask questions that have no answers, *I* get angry and frustrated. That is when I remind myself that it is better to give her a piece of my heart than a piece of my mind."

"Oh, I agree. Why, I bite my tongue so often, it's a minor miracle that I can talk at all." Snickering, Ella lisped, "Ithn't eathy to thpeak with a fat, thwollen tongue!"

Anna laughed, too. "Oh, you are a blessing," she said, giving her sister a sideways hug.

Ella's smile dimmed. "It isn't like we expect her to hire a pilot to drag a big sign behind his plane that says, 'I appreciate my daughters!'"

The Blessings Jar

"Like the ones that fly over Deep Creek Resort? Oh, I can almost see her, putting in her order."

In the kitchen, Ella helped herself to a mug of coffee. "You amaze me, Anna. Always cheerful, always thankful, no matter what mean-spirited thing *Maem* says or does."

Filling her own mug, she said, "You wouldn't say that if you could read minds. I spend a lot of time on my knees, asking forgiveness for the terrible things I think."

"So what do you think of *Maem*'s latest plot… inviting the Badens to Thanksgiving dinner."

"I hated the idea at first." She pictured David, looking sweet and sincere as he said he wished he could do more to help. "But it has grown on me."

"Oh, Anna," Ella said, her voice matching the dreamy look on her face, "I've been hoping and praying it is God's will for you two to get together one day. Who knows? It might happen, and you can give thanks for it next Thursday!"

"Reminds me of a quote I read a long time ago. 'Great love and great achievements require great risk.' I can't recall who said it, but it fits this situation perfectly."

"What risk? David thinks the world of you, and you feel the same way."

To explain, Anna would need to tell Ella about his past. She trusted her sister to keep it to herself, but if one day he asked how many others knew about it, she didn't want to lie.

"Goodness. Look at the time. I need to get to the diner, make sure Matthew and Luke have everything under control. We've been swamped since the harvest festival started."

"I'm busier than usual, too, some the result of curiosity-seekers, checking out how Pleasant Valley differs from Old Order Amish communities, and many referrals from my latest bride." She tugged her *kapp* into place. "And speaking of Matthew, is it a problem if I invite him to share Thanksgiving dinner with us?"

"Of course he is welcome, but doesn't he usually spend holidays with his brother and family?"

"They are traveling to Lancaster to visit a cousin, and Matthew said he'd stay behind to mind the farm."

"That doesn't surprise me at all."

The Blessings Jar

Shoulders lifted in a girlish shrug, Ella said, "I'm looking forward to it. Even made myself something brand new to wear, using material left over from Charity's dress. But please say nothing to *Maem*. I have already asked forgiveness for my sin of vanity!"

If the idea of spending time with Matthew made Ella happy enough to want to look pretty for him, Anna was all for it.

"Your secret is safe with me."

"By Tuesday, I will have filled all of my orders, so on Wednesday, I can go to the house and start getting things ready."

"What things?"

"I know how fussy you are about keeping the place clean and tidy, but I can give everything a quick going-over. Then…"

As Ella paced the kitchen, it seemed she was thinking out loud:

"The stuffing can be made ahead of time. The baked beans, too. And the mashed potatoes. Broccoli-cauliflower salad. Green beans. And the pies. I'll come back first thing Thursday morning, and while you're getting the turkey into the oven, I will set the table. That way, we can relax and enjoy some time together until you have to make the gravy and your biscuits." She stopped walking to say, "Oh, Anna, won't it be wonderful?"

She hadn't seen Ella this happy or excited since the morning of her wedding. Anna couldn't help herself. Gathering Ella in a sisterly hug, she said, "Yes, I think you're right."

Stepping back, Ella took Anna's hands in her own. "We must pray, pray, pray that *Maem* will not do or say anything to spoil the day."

"You're right again."

She rooted around in her tiny hand-stitched satchel. "Take my car to the diner." Closing Anna's fingers around her keys, she said, "Later, I'll bring *Maem* and *Daed* in the van."

Anna started to protest, then said, "Just enough time to stop by Red Oak Farm and order a nice fat bird."

Ella wiggled her eyebrows. "I hope David will take the order!"

From your lips to God's ears, Anna thought.

He was in the pen nearest the road when she arrived, squatting to lavish affection on Broze. Isaac was in there, too, petting another turkey. And outside the enclosure, David's dog raced back and forth, alter-

The Blessings Jar

nately yipping and barking.

"Patience, boy," he said.

He noticed her then, standing a few yards behind the pup.

"No need to be afraid. He's all bark, no bite."

She kept her eyes on the dog that continued leaping and yapping to get Isaac's attention. "Actions speak louder than words."

"Now, now," he said, chuckling, "you can't judge a book by its cover."

"It must be true, then… that love is blind."

"What's that you're holding?"

Anna glanced at the napkin-covered basket in her hands. "Couldn't sleep last night, and rather than waste time, I did a little baking." Truth was, she'd baked dozens of cookies, a pie, applesauce cake, and banana bread.

"I hope you like banana bread," she said, extending her arms a bit.

He waved her closer. The dog had settled down, but by now, the pen pulsed with putt-putting, clucking turkeys.

"If you come here, I'll break off a corner, so you can taste-test it."

A smile twinkled in his eyes, and he crossed the space between them in four long strides.

"Rumors about them are groundless. Especially these."

"That's a shame."

One brow rose. "Oh?"

"I came here to order one. For Thanksgiving dinner. It seems cruel to ask you to kill creatures that you're so fond of."

David took a step closer. "There are three—just three—that I consider pets. The rest?" He rubbed his thumb and fingertips together. "They pay the bills. I can't afford to get attached to them."

It made sense. Perfect *business* sense.

"Were you serious about that taste-test?"

Anna pulled back a corner of the napkin, and he held up his hands, like a man being held at gunpoint.

"I haven't washed, so if you wouldn't mind…"

She pinched off a bite-sized chunk, held it out. But instead of accepting it, he stepped closer still and, eyes closed and open-mouthed, waited to be fed, like a baby bird. Anna didn't know what possessed her to do it, but that's exactly what she did.

A crumb clung to his lower lip, and she brushed it away. The spontaneous action was intimate and innocent, sweet and ardent. Is that what marriage to him might be like? she wondered. *If it be Your will, Lord. Please, let it be Your will!*

"That was delicious," he said, interrupting her silent prayer. "Now about this turkey you want… any idea how many pounds?"

"Well, I am not sure, exactly. Are you aware that our mothers have put their heads together and decided that our families will share Thanksgiving dinner?"

He nodded. "I am."

Anna couldn't tell from his noncommittal reply whether or not he liked the plan.

"There will be ten of us gathered at our table," she continued. "At the diner, I serve half-pound portions. I cook for a hundred or more people every week, and that's why I order breast meat, drumsticks, and thighs in twenty- and thirty-pound orders. We only need one bird for our dinner, so what size turkey do you recommend?"

"I think a fifteen-pound bird will do. Unless you have plans to make soup or stew or sandwiches with the leftovers."

"Yes, I would like that."

"In that case, I'll choose a fat eighteen-pounder for you. Unless you would rather pick one, yourself."

"No!"

"Why?"

"It would be like eating a pet!"

He laughed, then said, "All right, then, I'll take care of it and bring it—ready for the roasting pan—on Wednesday."

"Thank you, David. I will pay you on Wednesday, then."

"You'll do no such thing! You're providing and preparing everything but pumpkin pies and whipped cream—your mother insisted—so consider the bird our contribution."

Anna nodded. "I should get to the diner. Ella will be there soon with my parents." She held out the banana bread. "It's delicious toasted, with butter…"

He held her gaze for what felt like a full minute before saying, "Thank you for the tip."

Oh, to have the power to read his mind!

"If we finish up here in time for lunch, Isaac and I will stop by the diner."

The Blessings Jar

"Good," she said, meaning it.

Balancing the bread plate on one big palm, he raised the other. "I will have washed up by then."

"Good," she said, and returned his playful smile.

While driving to the diner, Anna thought about the precious moments she'd just spent with him. After her rude outburst, he would have had every right to withdraw, even ignore her entirely. Instead, his behavior had been warmer, friendlier than before.

"Wishful thinking," she muttered, "or the answer to prayer?"

CHAPTER 10

"I won't apologize for showing up so late," he said, hugging the wrapped turkey to his chest, "because it would be a lie. I like being alone with you."

A shy smile turned up the corners of her mouth as he walked into the kitchen.

"We'll have to put it in the downstairs refrigerator," she said, opening the basement door. "Ella was here all day, cooking and baking, and there isn't room in this one for a muffin!"

He followed Anna down the stairs. "Did I hear correctly? Matthew will join us for dinner tomorrow?"

"Yes, and I can't remember the last time Ella looked forward to something this much."

He bent to slide the bird onto the empty top shelf. Straightening, he faced her and used his thumb to trace the contour of her jaw. "I know how she feels."

Even in the dim light of the bare overhead bulb, he could see that she was blushing. Anna turned her back to him and made her way back to the stairs.

"I made cocoa. You can stay and have a cup with me, can't you?"

"Real cocoa? Not powdered hot chocolate?"

"My own recipe," she said, leading the way into the kitchen. "Cocoa, sugar, butter, cream…"

He pressed a palm to his chest. "Be still my heart!"

Laughing, Anna filled two big mugs with the steaming chocolate drink and plopped a generous dollop of whipped cream atop each.

"Relax," she said, and slid a plate of chocolate chip cookies onto the table.

He sat down and helped himself to a cookie. "What time is dinner tomorrow?"

"Three o'clock. Our mothers' decision, not mine."

"Those two. Alone, they are a handful. Together?" He shook his head.

She joined in his laughter, and they spent the next minutes talking about his work and hers, the good results of her parents' recent doctor's visit, the uncharacteristically warm, clear weather, and how it was probably a precursor to heavy wet snow, piled high alongside the roadways.

The house was warm and quiet. David felt almost as at home here as he did in his own kitchen. She'd painted the room a butter-yellow with bright white trim that matched the cabinets. A big braided rug, centered beneath the round oak table, helped mute the sounds of spoons, clanking against stoneware. Evidence of Ella's cooking frenzy lingered in the air. Even the ticking clock and Mouser, purring on his lap, soothed him.

"I can put her in the other room."

"As long as she doesn't steal my cookie, she's fine right where she is."

Anna reached for a snickerdoodle, the same one David had grasped. He turned his wrist, just enough to break it down the middle, and they shared another moment of companionable laughter.

"Tell me, Anna, are you happy?"

She blinked a few times. "Why wouldn't I be?"

The Blessings Jar

"No reason. It's just... you smile more often these days."

"So do you."

"Really?"

"Really. And are you happy, David?"

"Yes," he said. Truth was, he was happier than he'd been in a long time. Happier, in fact, than he'd ever been.

He sipped his cocoa. "Can I ask you something?"

"Depends..."

Did she have any idea how much he loved that impish grin?

"Those things you said that night..." He leaned forward slightly, folded both hands on the table. "What, exactly, do you know?"

She heaved a shaky sigh.

Should have kept my big mouth shut. Because the question hadn't just erased her beautiful smile, it chilled the warm atmosphere, as well.

"I feel silly and stupid, admitting this, but I don't know anything, except you were a happy, mischievous boy until you were fifteen. And then you weren't."

Pleasant Valley's population couldn't compare with the city, but there were a few residents he'd only met in passing. Had she been one of those?

But wait... Even if that was the case, she couldn't have known what happened, not when she'd only been seven or eight at the time.

David decided to leave well enough alone and never to ask the question again. He didn't know if he could live with knowing she'd witnessed even one second of the crushingly degrading scenes in the schoolhouse... in the deacon's cold, dark cellar.

He drained his mug. "Think the cocoa is still hot?"

Anna delivered a refill. "There," she said, "that should warm you up."

She had no way of knowing that he didn't need cocoa for that. She'd thawed his frozen heart, warmed his entire world, just by being Anna.

One day soon, he'd tell her that. He'd tell her that he loved her, that he'd always loved her...

...and hoped it would be enough to convince her to spend the rest of her life with a man who is—what had her mother called him?—tainted.

The Blessings Jar

∼

Anna had never liked being in the basement. Particularly not at night. Especially not alone. Scrubbing and organizing had eliminated spiders and ants, but not even painted walls and area rugs on the concrete floor could turn the cave-like space into something it wasn't.

Think about something pleasant, she told herself, *or you'll never get this laundry finished.*

She thought of the many tourists who'd come to the diner tired and hungry, and left feeling energized, and looking forward to another visit to Pleasant Valley. Their enthusiastic chatter about the mountain views, rides on the old Baldwin steam locomotive, visits to the Our Town Theater and the Museum of Transportation made Anna wish for enough time—and the freedom—to enjoy some of the sights and activities, right in her own back yard.

Anna wondered how many of the local attractions David had seen.

None, probably, because for as long as she'd known him, he'd devoted himself to Red Oak Farm. And when the business faltered, he'd dedicated even more time and energy to saving it. Despite the trauma he'd survived, his efforts had saved the Badens' house and land, and the reputation of the generations-old family name.

He was everything a man ought to be, and more, and oh, how she wanted him for her own!

A chill wrapped around her. *This horrible place,* she thought, pulling a sheet out of the dryer. It had been smart, investing in three complete bedding sets for her parents' room. Elmer rarely had an accident, but Fannie's spinal cord injury had cut the nerves that connected her bladder to her brain. Her stubborn refusal to use a catheter caused a variety of problems, including frequent diaper changes and sodden linens. The moisture alarm had worked… until Fannie complained when Anna showed up at all hours of the night to replace damp sheets with dry ones. It meant linens in the washer and dryer at all hours of the day, but Anna refused to grumble about it. At least, not out loud.

She added the folded sheet to the stack, and recalled David's reaction the other night… her mother's unkempt, uncapped hair, the overturned night table, rumpled blankets and pillows tossed haphazardly to the floor, and the bent lampshade beside the bed. His wary expression made it clear that he didn't believe any of it had been an acci-

The Blessings Jar

dent, but to his credit, he quickly composed himself and asked how he could help. Anna had been mortified when her mother demanded that he leave, but yet again, he remained calm and respectful, and said goodbye, but not before cleaning the kitchen, to surprise her.

Something heartbreaking and horrible hit like a hard slap:

If by some miracle David *did* want to marry her, she couldn't say yes. She could never, ever say yes, because she loved him too much to burden him with the nonstop care of her parents… in particular, her rude, ungrateful mother.

Anna slumped onto an unused dining room chair, stored in the basement since the renovations happened, and wept.

CHAPTER 11

David's mother asked for a tour of the house, and Anna walked her through the rooms.

"It is so much more beautiful than I imagined. It is a surprise. A pleasant surprise."

"Oh? Why is that?"

"Before the accident, Fannie and I went back and forth between our houses so much that Robert teased us, said if we kept it up, we would wear a rut in the road. But in the two years since? Your mother has not invited me here, not once. Naturally, I assumed it was because things here were… less than pleasant."

Was there anyone who hadn't been hurt by Fannie's selfish behavior?

"You're welcome, any time," Anna said. "And you never need an invitation."

The Blessings Jar

"What a sweet thing to say." Charlotte looked around the big country kitchen. "Just look at this table," she said. "I have seen pictures in decorating magazines that aren't as lovely."

"Ella gets the credit," Anna said. "She has many talents."

"A family trait, then. Those rooms you created for your parents could just as easily be featured in one of those magazines."

"Charlotte!" Fannie called from the next room. "Charlotte, where are you?"

"Right here, old friend. I asked Anna to show me your apartment. You and Elmer must be so pleased. A place that offers privacy, where you can get around on your own. A body can't help but be impressed."

"Walls, windows, floors, and ceilings," Fannie said. "We are protected from nature's wrath, and that is enough."

Charlotte walked to the window and stood out of Fannie's line of sight. She met Anna's eyes and, shaking her head, mouthed, "*I am sorry…*"

"Where is Robert? And your sons?" Fannie asked. Facing Anna, she snapped, "You forgot to tell them that we are eating at three, didn't you?"

"She told them," Charlotte answered. "A bear tore up one of the outbuildings last night, and they had to make some repairs. Had to make sure the rest of the buildings are secure, in case the beast returns. It is only two-thirty. There is still time."

"Well," Fannie huffed, "it is that time of year when bears wander, trying to fatten up for their long winter's sleep. I am surprised they were not prepared for that."

Anna aimed the wheelchair toward the apartment. "Let's make sure you're ready for the meal."

And Fannie, knowing her daughter meant to check her diaper—and change it if needed—said, "We can do that later. Right now, I am fine." She made an attempt to engage the wheel lock.

Anna knew what *that* meant: Her mother intended to wait until everyone was seated, enjoying the meal, to announce that she needed help.

"But Fannie, if you don't let her take you now, she will have to get up from the table to do it later. Anna deserves to enjoy dinner as much as anyone. You agree, right?"

The Blessings Jar

Her mother pouted and said nothing as Anna wheeled her into the apartment. Said nothing as Anna made sure everything was clean and dry. Said nothing as they returned to the kitchen.

"Look," Charlotte said, "all of my boys are here, with ten minutes to spare!" She went to them, pressed a kiss to each winter-rosy cheek. "Is everything all right at home?"

"All is well, *Maem*," David said, looking at Anna. Looking… and aiming a loving smile her way.

"Everything's ready," Ella announced. "And Matthew brought apple cider!"

"We'll warm it up and serve it with dessert," Anna said. She faced David to say, "Will you carve the turkey?"

It took him no time to do the job, and at three minutes past three, he placed the big platter in the middle of the table.

Once everyone was seated, Elmer said, "Let us take a moment to thank *Gott* for those gathered and for providing this bounty."

After a moment of complete silence, he said a loud and resounding, "Amen!"

Bowls, platters, biscuit baskets, and laughter traveled up and down the table.

"I know I'm an outsider here," Matthew said, "but I wonder if I might make a suggestion."

"An outsider? Ridiculous!" Anna said. "You are family, so go ahead and suggest away!"

"When I was a boy in Lancaster, the family had a tradition. Each person had to name one thing they were thankful for, from the oldest to the youngest." Turning to Ella, who sat beside him, he said, "May I start?"

"I think that's a splendid idea," Elmer said. "And yes, you may start."

"I am grateful to be included here today." He faced Ella again. "But what I am thankful for is *you*."

Blushing, she said, "I am thankful for you, too."

Ethan, Charlotte, Robert, and Isaac spoke in turn, followed by Elmer.

"Fannie," he said, "you're next."

Anna tensed, wondering what cruel and vindictive thing her *maem* might say.

The Blessings Jar

"I am thankful for my husband and daughters, but especially Anna, who has sacrificed her happiness to see to the needs of her father and me."

A hush fell over the table. She'd surprised everyone, it seemed, but none more than

Anna. Was it a sign that in time, her mother could welcome David into their family?

By rights, it was her turn next. Could she do it without crying?

Yet again, it was David to the rescue. "I am thankful," he said, "that God has provided all of us with *enough*."

"Yes," Elmer said, nodding. "And Anna?"

She took a deep breath, then met David's eyes to say, "I am thankful, so very thankful, to have all of you in my life."

Half an hour later, the women gathered plates, flatware, and empty side dish bowls, and carried them to the far side of the kitchen, and left the men to talk work and hunting. Fannie scraped plates into the trash can, Ella wrapped up the leftovers, and Charlotte sat on a stool near the chopping block, plucking meat from the turkey carcass. "Will you make soup or stew with this, Anna?"

Rinsing the dish she'd just washed, Anna looked out the window, and saw Ella and Matthew making their way down the path. "Both," she said. "I'll start with soup, then thicken the broth and make stew from what's left."

"With your biscuits?"

"To serve with the soup, yes." She noticed that Ella and Matthew had drawn closer to one another. "Dumplings for the stew."

"Would you mind sharing your biscuit recipe?"

Now, she saw that her friend had taken her sister's hand, and the sight filled her with such joy, that tears sprung to her eyes.

"Anna," Charlotte said, "are you all right?"

"Splashed a little soapy water in my eye," she fibbed. And after drying her hands, Anna reached into the cupboard for her recipe box and slid a blank 3 x 5 card from the back of the stack. She sat across from Charlotte, explaining as she wrote:

ANNA'S BUTTERMILK BISCUITS

Ingredients:

The Blessings Jar

    2-1/4 cups cake flour
    2-1/4 cups all-purpose flour
    1-1/2 teaspoons salt
    1-1/2 tablespoons baking powder
    1 teaspoon baking soda
    1 cup cubed butter (very cold)
    2 cups buttermilk
    1/2 cup flour (for dusting and rolling)
    2 tablespoons melted butter (for biscuit tops)

Directions:

Preheat oven to 475°.

In large bowl, combine dry ingredients.

Cut in the butter until mixture is crumbly.

Add buttermilk and mix just until combined. (Dough will be slightly sticky.)

Turn dough onto a floured surface, and pat into a horizontal rectangle, about 1-1/2" thick.

Fold the left side of the rectangle over the right side and pat it out into a vertical rectangle.

Fold the bottom half up to the top, and press it out into a horizontal rectangle again.

Repeat the steps above 3 times for a total of 6 folds, taking care not to overwork the dough. (Folding is what creates the pretty layers.)

If dough starts feeling sticky, sprinkle a little flour on the layers, pat gently, and handle the dough lightly.

After 6 folds, gently pat the dough into a rectangle that is about 1" thick. Using a sharp circle biscuit cutter, press through the dough. Do not twist the cutter.

Place biscuits on parchment-covered baking sheet.

Brush melted butter onto tops of biscuits.

Bake at 475° for 5 minutes.

Reduce heat to 425°; bake an additional 8–10 minutes.

Remove from oven, and allow to sit 2–3 minutes before serving.

Serve warm.

"I don't know if I have the culinary talent to make them," Charlotte said.

"You do. But just between you and me? My first time, they turned out horribly because I overworked the dough. Just do what I did: Buy

The Blessings Jar

plenty of ingredients and keep making biscuits until a batch turns out well."

Ella and Matthew returned. "What's so funny?" Matthew asked.

"We're sharing recipes," Anna said.

"Your biscuits?" Ella laughed. "Anna's right: Practice makes perfect. Why, even I can make them now!"

Charlotte said, "Fannie, old friend, you are blessed with two wonderful daughters."

"You are blessed, too, with two wonderful sons, and Isaac."

Anna couldn't help but wonder if her mother was setting Charlotte up for a caustic comment.

"I have behaved poorly, but my girls—and Elmer, too—have stood by me. God in heaven knows I do not deserve their loving support." She began to cry, and squeaked out, "I hope they can forgive me, and that they will believe it when I say things are going to change!"

Charlotte, Ella, and Anna got onto their knees around Fannie's wheelchair and hugged her. They were laughing and crying and talking nonstop when David crossed the room, carrying a stack of dessert plates.

"Brought you a few more dirty dishes," he said. Then, "Hey. Why is everyone crying?"

"Don't worry, son," Charlotte said, "these are happy tears."

"Happy tears?" he echoed. "I never heard of such a thing." He put the plates into the sudsy water and backed out of the room, hands up and eyes wide. "If this is how you ladies look when you're happy, I don't want to be around when you're sad."

Anna knew exactly what she'd add to her blessings jar tonight:

"There is *a chance. There is really a chance!"*

CHAPTER 12

It was the day before Christmas Eve, and thanks to back-to-back snowstorms and busier-than-normal work schedules, Anna hadn't seen David since Thanksgiving. And despite occasional "how are you" phone calls, she missed him. Oh, how she missed him!

She'd thrown herself into preparing the diner, so that she could shutter the place tomorrow and the day after.

Shortly before Thanksgiving, she'd made space near the cash register for Polly's beadwork. Tourists and non-Amish diners alike bought up the trinkets, in no small part because Anna had suggested a small sign: *Stocking Stuffers*.

She'd also agreed to let local artisans hang pictures of their handicrafts on the *Let's All Eat* bulletin board.

In past years, the months between the Harvest Festival and the Spring Fling were, as Elmer liked to say, "Slower than molasses in

February." But Anna's changes had paid off handsomely.

"If this becomes a trend," her father said, "you might be able to take some time off."

"What she should do," Fannie put in, "is research assisted living centers, where the two of us can get the care we need, and give her a chance at a full, happy life."

"*Maem*! What a thing to say. I can't do that!"

"You can, and you should."

Anna sat on her heels between them. "Where is this coming from all of a sudden?"

"We've been talking about it for weeks," her father said.

"Weeks?" She looked up at her mother. "But… aren't you happy at home?"

"The way you care for us, we couldn't be anything *but* happy!" Fannie said.

This was a dream. It had to be. How else could she explain this crazy turn of events? Anna had never so much as considered moving them into a facility, not when they nearly toppled down the basement stairs while learning to maneuver their wheelchairs, not when they

The Blessings Jar

fussed during their daily exercises, not when they got pneumonia at the same time, and she couldn't see herself doing it now.

"Will you at last think about it, *süßes mädchen*?"

"I will *pray* about it," she told them. "But right now, it's time to go home so you can rest."

Elmer reached for Fannie's hand and, smiling, she took it.

"We're not tired, but you no doubt are. So yes, let's go home."

Something peculiar was going on here, and Anna wasn't sure she wanted to find out what. She'd just slid two trays of cookies into the oven when headlights, glinting from the toaster, caught her attention. She set the timer and went to the door.

"David," she said, opening it wide, "are you mad, driving around at this hour, in a snowstorm?"

"I suppose I am a little mad... about you."

First chance she got, Anna would call Dr. Emily to find out if madness was contagious. Because if so, that might explain his out of the blue comment and her parents' peculiar behavior too.

He winked, then hung up his coat and hat, and poured himself a cup of coffee. Carrying it to the table, he scanned the sea of cookies that covered every flat surface.

"For the diner?"

"Some of them, yes. And for your family, and Matthew's, and—"

"Say, have you heard? His brother isn't coming back to Pleasant Valley."

"Never?"

"That's right," he said around a mouthful of cookie.

"But what about the house? And the farm? And all that equipment?"

"He gave it to Matthew." He took another bite. "Repayment for the thousands of dollars and hundreds of hours Matthew put into the place."

"What will they do in Lancaster? And those sweet children… Charity says they're doing so well in school!"

"They have teachers in Pennsylvania, too, you know."

"Well, of course they do, but…" She groaned. "Why does it seem everyone wants to move elsewhere all of a sudden?"

"Just Mark and Mary, to my knowledge."

"And my parents."

The Blessings Jar

"Anna. Stop pulling my leg. They are wheelchair bound. Where could they go?"

"To an assisted living center. Believe me, I was just as shocked when they sprung the idea on me a little while ago."

He helped himself to a sugar cookie. "That makes no sense. For two years now, you've taken excellent care of them."

"I thought so, too." The timer beeped, and after removing the pastry sheets from the oven, Anna had a cookie, too.

"Give them a day or two. They'll change their minds."

"They've been thinking about this for weeks. Weeks, David!"

When Anna looked over at him, he was smiling.

"What's so funny?"

"I've heard of sparkling eyes before. But sparkling lips?" He went to her, used a fingertip to dust red sugar crystals from her mouth. "I hope you'll forgive me, but I just have to know…"

He kissed her, and she let him.

"I was right. You *do* taste as good as you look."

His smile vanished, quick as the smoke from a spent match. "Anna, *meine süße* Anna, I didn't mean to make you cry."

"You… you didn't."

He led her to the table, sat on the nearest chair, and pulled her onto his lap. "If I didn't make you cry, then what did?"

It all tumbled out… her feelings of guilt, her hope that it was God's will for the two of them to be together, that saddling him with paralyzed in-laws was unfair and merciless…

"*Süße, süße* Anna," he said. "Shh. Nothing in this world can keep us apart. Don't you know that by now?"

"But David, you have no idea how hard it can be, taking care of—"

"What I don't know, you will teach me. All the rest will fall into place."

"How can you be so sure?"

"Because I love you."

"*Why?*"

"Because," he said again, "you gave me back my life, my dignity, and self-respect." He gave her shoulders a gentle shake. "You saved me."

Anna rested her head on his shoulder.

"Would you like your Christmas gift now or in the morning?"

The Blessings Jar

"My…" Using her apron hem, she dried her eyes. "You came here to give me a present?"

"Isn't that what Christmas Eve is for?" He put her on her feet, then turned her around, and eased her onto the chair. "Don't go anywhere."

Funny, but she hadn't noticed him carrying a sack into the house. He handed it to her, and pulled a second chair close to hers. "Well, aren't you going to open it?"

Whatever was inside was heavy and hard, with sharp edges. Anna peeked into the bag, and withdrew a tin foil-wrapped package, tied up with a red ribbon. She found the seam and pulled at it, and revealed four leather-bound books: *Treasure Island, The Secret Garden, The Old Man and the Sea,* and *A Christmas Carol*.

She hugged them to her chest. "Oh, David, they're wonderful."

"Look inside this one," he said, tapping *A Christmas Carol*.

"'To my one and only Anna,'" she read aloud. And it was signed, *Love, David*.

Love? Maybe *now* she was dreaming!

"I have something for you, too. Should I get it now?"

"Well, yeah!" he said, and took another cookie.

"They're downstairs." She hurried to the basement door. "Don't go anywhere."

Masculine laughter followed her down the steps, and when she got back to the kitchen, he was at the stove, refilling his cup.

"Took you long enough."

She handed him the biggest gift first, then sat smiling as its bright red wrapper fluttered to the floor.

"A painting... of *me*?"

Anna only nodded.

"But how did you find the time?"

"A person makes time for the things—and the people—that matter."

"But it's such a good likeness. How did you do it, when we Amish have no photographs, and I didn't, you know, *pose*?"

"The image of you is imprinted on my brain, on the inside of my eyelids. I see you when I blink, when I sleep."

He stared at the picture. "It's... it's like looking in a mirror. Just wait until my mother sees it. She wondered if you were still painting."

"I'm glad you like it. Would you like your other gift now?"

The Blessings Jar

"Two presents? But I only gave you one."

"Just because you wrapped the books together doesn't lessen the number." She held out the second gift, and this time, watched as shiny gold paper sailed to the floor.

"A jar?"

"A blessings jar."

He unscrewed the lid, plucked a slip of paper from it. "'He is beautiful,'" David read. On the second slip, she'd written, "'One day, God willing, he'll be mine.'"

"Anna," he whispered, "this whole jar, it's filled with things like this?"

Reaching into her pocket, she said, "Read this one next."

David took his time, unfolding it. "'Will you be in my life, forever?'"

"Does it mean… are you… is this a… a proposal?"

This time when she nodded, his eyes grew damp.

"I get it now."

"Get what?"

"What 'happy tears' means."

David got to his feet, pulled her close.

"By the way?"

She blinked away tears of joy.

"Yes, I'll be in your life, forever."

And, as if to seal it *forever,* he kissed her long and well.

ABOUT THE AUTHOR

Once upon a time, *USA Today* best-selling author Loree Lough sang for her supper, performing before packed audiences throughout the U.S. and Canada. Now and then, she blows the dust from her 6-string to croon a tune or two for the "grandorables," but mostly, she writes. (And writes.) Her stories have earned thousands of 5-star reviews, hundreds of industry and "Readers' Choice" awards, and 7 book-to-movie options. At last count, nearly 17,000,000 copies of Loree's books were in circulation, and by year-end of 2022, she'll have 146 books on the shelves. She and her husband split their time between a home in the Baltimore suburbs and a cabin in the Allegheny Mountains, where she continues to hone her "identify the critter tracks" skills.

http://www.loreelough.com

Progressive Rising Phoenix Press is an independent publisher. We offer wholesale pricing and multiple binding options with no minimum purchases for schools, libraries, book clubs, and retail vendors. We offer substantial discounts on bulk orders and discounts on individual sales through our online store. Please visit our website at:

www.ProgressiveRisingPhoenix.com

If you enjoyed reading this book, please review it on Amazon, B & N, or Goodreads.
Thank you in advance!

www.ingramcontent.com/pod-product-compliance
Lightning Source LLC
LaVergne TN
LVHW010300260326
834688LV00044B/1376